Year of the Dragon

The Dragon Manifesto 2

Kathleen H. Nelson

Year of the Dragon

The Dragon Manifesto 2

Kathleen H. Nelson

Paperback ISBN 978-1-77400-056-4
Ebook ISBN 978-1-77400-057-1

www.dragonmoonpress.com

DEDICATION

To Les,
Thank you for turning our life together into an epic poem.
I'll go adventuring with you any day.

ACKNOWLEDGMENTS

Thank you, Gwen.

CHAPTER 1

Mara was sitting up in bed, drawing dragons in her journal—the real, live, fire-breathing kind! The kind that Roz had introduced her and Max to just a few short days ago! The memory both boggled and delighted her. They had fraternized with dragons! How insanely cool was that? She quick-sketched Quetzalcoatl's head: those rheumy, heavy-lidded eyes, the saurian jawline, that fabulous, almost Elizabethan frill. According to Roz, the drakena had been worshipped as a god in her early years. Mara could think of worse things to adore.

A grainy snore leapt up from the other side of the bed: Max sleeping off the last vestiges of a two-day hangover. Despite being a self-confessed light-weight when it came to hard liquor, he had knocked back glass after glass of high-octane Scotch in the hours after their meeting with the dragons. Brigit had gleefully egged him on! 'G'won, charaid, ave a'nother, it'll steady yer nerves!'

As if corrupting Roz hadn't been enough!

She drew a mean little portrait of the Scottish drakena, giving her exes for eyes like they did in the comics to convey drunkenness. She knew she was being petty and maybe even a little jealous, but it just wasn't fair! When Brigit wanted something, she reached right out and grabbed it—and too bad if it belonged to someone else!

What if she made a grab for Max?

Max snarked again, louder this time. Oddly enough, Mara found the sound reassuring. No dragon was going to lure this darling bagpipe of a man away from her. He was hers and hers alone.

She flipped to a fresh page in her journal and began sketching the smallest of the drakena that they had met. Sadie was a snowball to Quetzalcoatl's avalanche, and little more than a fairy compared to Brigit. Even so, Mara had feared her at first for she had a hard, hungry look about her, the kind of look that didn't see anything wrong with man-eating. Then she and Max fed her a chunk of roasted pork and everything changed. Instead of potential foodstuffs, they became caterers. Mara considered that a win. Max wasn't so sure.

Max began to saw wood in earnest. Mara reached for the remote, intending only to damp down the lumberjack sounds with low-volume TV twitter. The late-night news spanned into view. The headline read: South Bay Tragedy. The image on the screen was of orange flames, flashing red lights, and arcing plumes of fuzzy white spray. A grim-faced reporter appeared in the foreground. "This is Michelle Kelsey," she said, "reporting live from the country home of local celebrity Aurora Vanderbilt."

"What?!?"

"Authorities say the fire started earlier this evening, most likely in the barn. They also have reason to believe that arson may be involved. No bodies have been found on the premises yet. However, that is not the end of this story."

Mara yelped again and then slugged Max in the arm. He lurched to consciousness in mid-snark, then flopped onto his back to squint at her. "S'up?" She made no reply; she was fixated on the television.

"A car registered to Ms. Vanderbilt was found crushed and burning at the bottom of a ravine in San Mateo," the reporter revealed. "Her whereabouts—and the whereabouts of her daughter, Rosalyn—are currently unknown. If you see either of them or know where they are, please contact the Saratoga police department. Likewise, if you have any information about this evening's accident on northbound 280 just past the Doran Bridge in Hillsborough, contact the California Highway Patrol—anonymously, if you prefer.

"Back to you, Kent."

"Shit!" Mara squawked, and lunged for her cell phone. Max scowled as if it pained him to process what he was seeing, and then touched her arm. "Who you calling, Mar?"

"Who do you think?" she fired back, as she scrolled for Roz's number.

"You sure that's a good idea?" he asked, trying to glance at the bedroom clock without seeming to. "It's late."

"What if it was your mother?" she fired back, as auto-dial did its thing. One ring, then another. C'mon, pick up! "Wouldn't you want to know about something like this ASAP?" Ring three and then a click, her call being shunted to message. "Dammit!" she hissed, and shook the phone like a ketchup bottle, trying to bully the signal into a more favorable configuration. Surprisingly enough, it seemed to work, because the message sheared off into a bleary, "Hello?"

"It's me, Mara," she said, not bothering to whisper since Max was on his side now, head propped in one hand and listening intently. "Where are you?"

"Bakersfield," Roz mumbled.

Mara hadn't known what she'd been expecting, but it sure wasn't that. Before she could stop herself, she blurted, "Why?"

"Truck's in the shop," Roz said, still groggy-sounding. "Rear axle snapped like a friggin' matchstick."

In the cellular background, Brigit sniffed. "Ye canna say A didn't give ye fair warning."

"Shut up," Roz said, and then abandoned the quarrel. "So what's up, Mar? Something tells me this isn't a midnight butt-dial."

Phoning had been a knee-jerk reaction, her version of fight or flight. But now that she had Roz on the line, the weightiness of the news that she was carrying settled against her diaphragm like a deep-sea anchor. "Uhm," she said, finding it hard to draw a full breath. "I don't suppose you caught the late-night news."

"Nah," Roz said, and cranked out a yawn. "I crashed early. Seemed like a good way to end a shitty day. Why?"

"Uhm." Mara didn't want to say. The words felt like broken glass in her mouth. But no matter how badly they cut her up, she was bound by best-friendship to spit them out. It. "Your house burned down tonight."

"What?!" It was a bolting-upright sound, alarm catapulted by surprise. A frantic, fabric-y pat-pat-pat followed, and then, "Where's my friggin' phone?"

"Tha one pressed tae yer ear?" Brigit queried from the peanut gallery.

"Shit," Roz said, and then, "Mara, lemme call you back, OK? I gotta talk to Mom."

A microsecond later, the line went dead.

Mara pressed the phone to her chest as if to share her heartache with the universe. As she sat there, dreading the immediate future, Max snaked an arm around her neck and gently guided her head onto the furry pillow of his chest. She didn't realize that she was crying until his chest hair turned slick.

"It's gonna be OK, Mar," he said, rocking her a little. "I'm sure Aurora is fine. She's probably not even back from her Seattle gig yet. And you know she can go for days without looking at her cell phone. She probably doesn't even know that people are looking for her."

She sniffed back tears, struggling with the comfort he was trying to give her. "But they said they found her car—"

He cut her off before she could plant an image that neither

of them wanted in their heads. "She leaves it at the Park and Fly when she travels. It was probably stolen."

She wanted to believe him, she really did. But she had this deep-down toe-curling sense that theft wasn't part of the equation this evening. Seriously, who in their right mind was going to steal a Pepto-pink sedan when there were so many other less eye-grabbing options available? "Do we know what time her flight was supposed to—"

Her cell dinged, resetting her focus. An instant after she hit 'Accept', Roz got right to the point. "Mom wasn't in the house when it went up, was she?"

"What? No!"

Roz did not seem to hear her. "I called three times," she said. "The call couldn't be completed. Why is that? Tell me, Mar. Was she there?"

"No, sweetie," Mara said softly, as if she were tiptoeing through a minefield, "she wasn't there." She paused for a moment, bracing herself for the impending explosion. "It looks like she was in an accident on her home from the airport."

The beginnings of relief poured out of Roz only to be strangled mid-sigh. "What? What the fuck, Mara! Why didn't you tell me? Is she OK?"

Mara balked, unwilling to hope or speculate. That's when Max stepped in. He had his phone out and was studying a news report that he had pulled up. "No one knows, Roz. The fire from the crash was so intense, the fire guys couldn't put in out. It could take weeks to find out if there are any—" The word stuck in his throat. He cleared it with a sorry little cough. "If there are any remains within. They're searching the grounds as well."

"You gotta be kidding me," Roz said, a dangerous mix of desperate and caustic. "This is some kind of sick joke, right?"

"I'm afraid not, sweetie," Mara said, feeling desolate and helpless.

"No, goddamnit," Roz snarled, and then bashed something on her end of the call. "I don't believe you. I won't! My mother is not dead!"

"We're holding out hope, too," Max said. "But you need to brace yourself just in—"

"My truck will be ready tomorrow morning," Roz said, all business and dry ice now. "I'll be back in town in time for supper."

"Plan on staying with us," Mara said. "You and Brigit can arm wrestle for the couch."

"Whatever," Roz said, so tight-jawed that that Mara could feel the tension over the phone. "I gotta go now. See you tomorrow."

With that, the line went dead again. Mara scrubbed the threat of tears out of her eyes with a knuckle and then curled up against Max, who was still looking at his phone. She usually loved his bookishness, but tonight, it galled her. "How can you read at a time like this?"

He pointed to the midsection of an article written in a really small font. "This says there might have been another car involved in Aurora's accident. The driver of that one is definitely dead."

"I can't believe this is happening," Mara said, and buried her face in his chest hair again. "What are we going to do?"

"There's nothing we can do at the moment, love," Max replied, gently stroking the back of her head. "Ours is to watch and wait—and hope."

CHAPTER 2

"This is Michelle Kelsey, reporting live from Saratoga."

Charles flipped the television in his bedroom off with a sullen click of the remote. He should have been happy or at least satisfied for having scratched two high-priest action items from his to-do list, but as it was all he could think of was the collateral damage. Local celebrity Aurora Vanderbilt. Her 'accident' was his doing. He had picked the time and the place. He had hired the driver. The only detail he hadn't anticipated was her taking her assassin out even as he killed her. What a woman! What a goddamn shame!

Restlessness swept him to his feet and toward the front of the house. He hadn't showered yet so he stank of smoke and adrenalized sweat, but he didn't care. It wasn't like he had anyone to impress—anymore. Besides, the front room absolutely reeked of stale drake musk and pool scum, which made him smell like a daisy by comparison. No way that stench was ever coming out of the walls. As soon as he wrapped up things here, he was either putting the place on the market—or burning it down.

His stomach growled as the kitchen spanned into view, but he wasn't hungry, not really, leastwise not for the half-eaten week-old chorizo burrito that was the fridge's sole occupant. He could go for a glass of wine, though—scant comfort to be sure but better than nothing and maybe he'd be able to sleep later. He pulled a random bottle from the crate that he kept on the counter only to choke up when he saw that it was a Monte Bello.

Their wine.

Tezcatlipoca would have ridiculed him for indulging such sentimentality—and rightly so. Charles was the Great One's high priest, a warrior for the natural order. The cause required him to do what needed to be done. No other option sufficed.

But it still sucked.

He walked his freshly poured glass into the front room. It was ruined, dragon-trashed. The only things that weren't broken, battered, water-logged, and-or stained were the pottery pieces that he'd salvaged from Quetzalcoatl's lair. They were grouped on the mantle like old spirits intent on warding off chaos. He strode over to the hearth to admire them. Their antiquity had excited Aurora. 'This would be a fabulous addition to any museum!' He had agreed, but only to make her happy. How he wished that he had packed more into that moment!

The sound of breaking glass in the background jarred him out of his thoughts. His first reaction was irritation: asshole! But even as he swiveled in that direction, ready to excoriate the idiot for his clumsiness, the familiar outlines of a sopping-wet mandrake slopped into view.

Shit. Wrong asshole.

Grishka Rasputin seemed more imposing than usual, fuller in the shoulders and less bent. He seemed to be moving better, too. Charles attributed the change in the mandrake's bearing to post-hunt endorphins. It never occurred to him that Grishka might still be on the hunt or that he was the drake's intended prey until Grishka seized him by the throat and thrust him into the air. For one stunned moment, Charles' mind went blank. All of his inner voices were silent except for the one shouting, what the fuck?

"You knew, didn't you?" Grishka rasped.

"Knew what?" Charles asked, and then gasped as Grishka pressed his hoary, ridiculously strong thumbs into Charles' windpipe.

"You knew they meant to kill Her!"

Charles knew exactly who 'Her' was. It only took him a split-second to decide to lie. "I was—only—told—to—locate her."

Grishka mocked the lie with a sneer. The short, sharp exhalation tingled as it hit Charles' face, promising an ugly rash later. If he lived that long. He could hold his breath for a couple of minutes when he was underwater, but that wasn't quite the same as having your air pinched off by an angry dragon. His pulse was starting to accelerate in his ears already, and the peripheries of his vision were fuzzy.

"Tezcatlipoca gave Drogo permission to do it, didn't he?" Grishka asked. "That was their plan all along."

Not—privy—to that—con-ver—sation," Charles croaked, the truth in its own twisted way. "Drogo—doesn't—like—me."

Grishka sneered again, a less caustic spray. "Another thing we have in common, aye, Carlito?" When Charles failed to acknowledge the commiseration, preferring instead to hoard his last few molecules of air, the mandrake made a warbling sound deep in his throat and then set Charles gently back on his feet. "Sometimes I forget how fragile your kind are," he said. Then, as Charles struggled to refill his lungs, he added, "Tezcatlipoca is fortunate to have you as his high priest. I should have known you would not betray him."

"Yo, dude! Got anything to eat?"

Both Charles and Grishka arched their necks and then craned their heads in the direction of the kitchen. The refrigerator door was open. The ass-end of a man girded in a bath towel was parked in front of the opening. "There's, like, nothing in here," Aldo complained, and then popped up, prairie-dog-like, with the half-eaten burrito in hand. "OK if I eat this? I'm starv—" He froze, stunned to momentary stillness by Grishka's imposing presence. Then he took a tyrannosaurus-sized bite from the burrito and said, "I wouldn't have pegged you as a night owl, dude, but it's cool. I can sleep through anything but a curtain call. I'll just take this—" He waved the burrito's remains like a piece of evidence in a murder trial. "To my room."

Grishka forestalled him with an outstretched hand. "Wait."

Then he turned to Charles and said, "Who is this man to you?"

It galled Charles to have to take responsibility for such a self-centered bumpkin, but since the bumpkin had knowledge that Charles needed, Charles felt obliged to protect him—at least for the opening round. But, if the drake pulled rank—see ya, stupido! "He's a new associate," he said. "He's going to help me hunt down Aurora's daughter."

"That's right!" Aldo said, spraying flecks of half-masticated burrito everywhere. "We're going to track her down and cap her ass and seize her dragon."

Idiot. Charles hadn't been planning to tell Grishka about the second drakena, leastwise not in a straight-up one-way giveaway. He cursed Aldo way under his breath and then brusquely shooed him toward the back of the house. "Go and get some sleep already. I want to start early tomorrow."

But even as Charles tried to get rid of him, Grishka motioned him into the front room with a come-hither frill of his fingers. Self-centered bumpkin or not, his survival instincts were spot-on. He tossed the now-empty burrito box back into the fridge, then shuffled out of the darkened kitchen and into the foyer. "Closer," Grishka insisted, when Aldo stalled well beyond Grishka's reach. Aldo took a few more baby steps. With a rare show of impatience, Grishka reached out and snagged the idiot by an arm, then hauled him close and snuffled him from ear to ear.

"I am curious," he said afterward. "What did you do to get yourself cursed?"

"What?" Aldo said, looking both appalled and affronted. "What are you talking about? I haven't done anything."

"I've only known him for a handful of hours," Charles said. "And I can already say with complete confidence that he definitely earned whatever wizardry he's wearing."

"It's not that strong," Grishka said, squinting as he studied the spell's outer structure. "But it was cast with passion." He ran a finger along the man's receding hairline and then asked, "Has your hair always been this sparse?"

Aldo reared back, then ran a hand over his shower-slick comb-over and said, "There's nothing wrong with my hair. It's wet, is all."

"If you say so," Grishka said, and then dismissed him with a brusque flick of the wrist. "That is all. Go now." A moment later, he barked, "Be gone!"

Aldo bolted, both hands clutching at his towel. Grishka watched as he passed through the kitchen and into the darkened reaches beyond, then shook his head like an old-timer who's seen something ridiculous and new. "I cannot begin to imagine what sort of use he could be to you."

Charles shrugged. "He knows the territory. Not only that, he's obsessed with finding the daughter—Aurora's daughter." Shit! That was the second time in as many minutes that he had said Aurora's name out loud without intending to. Was Grishka subliminally goosing him into it? "She seems to have gone underground. If this guy can help me dig her up faster for the price of a half-eaten chorizo burrito, then so much the better. You know how patient Tezcatlipoca is."

Grishka rumbled, appreciating the joke. Suddenly, he was quite glad that he had decided not to kill The Great One's high priest. This human made life a bit more entertaining. Which was not to say that he was above pressing an advantage when it landed in his lap. "Does the Great One know about the daughter's drakena?"

"Absolutely," Charles said, because one did not withhold that kind of information from Tezcatlipoca. If anything, one gave him as many updates as possible and then left him to put the pieces together whatever way that he wanted them. "He wants me to knock her out and bring her back to the compound so he can copulate with her."

"Is that the way it needs to be?" Grishka asked then. "Have none of the foundlings sexed properly?"

"That's what Drogo Channing says," Charles said, happy for the change of subject. "I overheard a phone conversation that he had with one of his thralls a few days ago. He said that Tezcatlipoca's pathway to the next age was crumbling like a clump of desiccated dragon shit, and that once he'd made the necessary arrangements, he was going to quit the conspiracy and pursue his own manifesto."

"Does Tezcatlipoca know this?" Grishka asked, toying with his beard as he digested what he had heard.

"Given Drogo's dislike of me, I did not think it wise to forward that information while he was still on the premises. But now that he's gone—" On impulse, he pulled out his cell. "I could call the Great One right now. You could give him the news. I'm sure he'd take it better from his most trusted advisor."

Grishka cast him a sideways glance and bared his yellowed teeth in a sly facsimile of a smile. "How generous of you to offer me the chance to give Tezcatlipoca bad news."

"You can't blame a guy for trying," Charles said, projecting insouciance even though he was inwardly regretting his attempt to play the drake.

"No? You think not?" Grishka asked, injecting a hint of menace into his tone. "I thought you knew dragons better than that." Then, just like that, he let Charles off the hook. "Had

I been on speaking terms with the Great One, I might have considered doing you that favor. As it is, I am furious with him for deceiving me about Quetzalcoatl's murder and mean to stay well away from him until the Divine graces me with the ability to forgive. You may tell him I said so."

Damn. Way to turn the tables, dragon. The only thing Charles could do was acknowledge the mastery of the move. "I should have known better than to try and sneak something past you, Grishka Rasputin. Delivering your message to him will be my just desserts. Is there anything else you would like him to know?"

Grishka gave him a critical once-over and then approved what he saw with a nod. "You are a worthy high priest, Carlito. I will ask the Divine to protect you. And when the Great One asks after my whereabouts, you can tell him I am looking for the runaway. You can tell him that I will contact him when I find her. But," he added, just as Charles started to relax, "you cannot tell him where I'll be."

"Not a problem," Charles said, "since I won't know."

"Oh, but you will," Grishka said, 'because I'll be staging my hunt from here. You will need to put more water in the pool and restock your meat locker. Acquire more vodka, too."

Charles shifted, seemingly to retrieve his long-forgotten wine glass but actually to hide the bad reaction he was having to the news. After all he had done and endured over the past few months, the absolute last thing he wanted was more draconic company and all the shit that that entailed. A break! He needed a break, the chance to be alone and let his humanity decompose.

"It must be hard for you," Grishka said, demonstrating again his eerie ability to read random thoughts.

"No," Charles said, because he could say nothing else, "it's no problem. Stay as long as you want."

"I was referring to Aurora," the mandrake pointed out. "She was a remarkable woman. It must have been hard for you to kill her. Do you look forward to finding her offspring? Or do you dread it?"

Charles felt a twinge in his chest—Grishka trying to goose him again. As if he needed to be prodded where Aurora was concerned. "So long as I get the job done," he said, surprised to find himself on the verge of snapping, "what do you care?"

Grishka flared his nostrils as if to analyze the sudden influx of hostility in the air. Then he broke out that sly pseudo-smile again and said, "I don't care, actually. I am just curious. And for me, there is no wondering without asking.

"I believe I will retire to the pool now to commune with the Divine. You can raise the water level tomorrow."

"Thanks," Charles said, not entirely succeeding in containing his sarcasm. Grishka did not seem to hear, though. He was already shambling down the hallway, transitioning back into a water dragon as he went. Good riddance, Charles thought, and returned to his twice-forgotten glass. The contents smelled of blackberries and forest floor. He was tempted to throw the whole thing into the fireplace. Instead, he sat down on the floor and savored every drop.

CHAPTER 3

Drogo's phone buzzed. Drogo ignored it until the call went to voice. The message was classic Tezcatlipoca—no greeting, no posturing, just a blunt, "Where are you?" As it happened, Drogo had just checked into a San Francisco hotel that catered to rich people and their privacy. He needed a place to stage the next phase of his plan to steal the next age. He was going to need refreshment, too, now that the rush from killing the Great One's sister was wearing off. Sweet Divinity! He had never consumed such a powerful lifeforce! Was that just the drakena—or did all former gods taste like that? If so, then making a run at Tezcatlipoca might be worth the risk. Killing him would be like eating the sun.

The thought made him drool.

But—first things first.

"Did you get the private jet?" he asked Aziz, whom Drogo had recently recruited to serve as his personal assistant. The lesser drake thought he was being groomed as a confidante. Drogo let him think what he would. "I refuse to be surrounded by hundreds of fetid, overfed humans for seventeen hours."

"I have hired a plane," Aziz replied, from the suite's work-cubby. "It will depart three days hence. Do you want—provisions?"

Drogo's perceptions shifted in the span of a blink, offering him the flipside of a plane full of overfed humans. Drool flooded back into his mouth, but practicality held firm.

"Nothing live," he said.

"I could drug them," Aziz said, in a dangling tone.

"I don't like the taste of sedated meat," Drogo said. "And if we didn't sedate them, we'd have to listen to them squealing until we got hungry. No," he went on, before Aziz could tempt him again, "we'll hunt before we board the plane and again when we land."

His phone buzzed again. Same caller. Same message, too, although more heated than the last. He debated ignoring this one, too, but then reminded himself that he was going to have to engage the Great One sooner or later.

"But why?" Aziz warbled, when Drogo reached for the phone. "We're done with him!"

"He doesn't need to know that," Drogo replied, and then tapped Tezcatlipoca's number. Tezcatlipoca answered almost immediately.

"About time!" the great drake snapped, in lieu of a greeting. "I've been calling for days! Where are you?"

"My location is none of your business," Drogo said, because anything more polite would have been unlike him and therefore suspicious. "I've done your bidding. Now I must look after my own affairs for a while."

"Is it true then?" Tezcatlipoca asked, not bothering to disguise the hunger in his tone. "You killed her?"

"Didn't your pet, Carlito, tell you?"

"Of course he told me," Tezcatlipoca said, snapping again. "But I wanted to hear it from you."

Of course. The great drake had hated his sister with a passion that bordered on weakness. He'd want a reliable confirmation of her demise—and all the gory details. A report from Carlito wouldn't have had the same visceral impact.

"I took her by surprise," Drogo said, sharing the memory simply because it excited him to recall it. "She fought me off for a brief time, but lacked the stamina needed to drive me away. An instant after she succumbed to her weakness, I

24

tore her throat out. Her lifeforce was—" He paused to relive that remembered rush of power. "Exhilarating. I have never experienced the like."

"Nor will you ever again," Tezcatlipoca said.

Don't be so sure of that!

Seemingly satisfied with the telling, the Great One jumped straight to the next thing on his mind. "Have you seen Rasputin? Is he there with you?"

Drogo hissed. As if he would spend one more second than absolutely necessary in the company of that pathetic excuse for a dragon! "No!" he said. "I sent him after the runaway last night and haven't seen him since. Why?"

"I need him to come here and help with the wyrms," Tezcatlipoca said. "But he's not answering my calls, either. Someone who didn't know any better might be tempted to think that the two of you are conspiring against me.

"So—are you?"

Coming out of the clear blue like that, the near-miss left Drogo a little shaken. Ancient or not, the great drake still had some savvy left in him. He knew he was vulnerable and that Drogo was ambitious. He was trying to decide which flank to protect. Drogo was suddenly glad that he had taken this call. Knowledge was power.

"You know that I despise that twisted creature," he said. "I would sooner conspire with a monkey."

"I thought as much," Tezcatlipoca said. "I just wanted to hear you say it."

"Hear this, too, then," Drogo said, seeing an opportunity to muddy up Rasputin's waters. "That honey-tongued freak wants you to believe that he is on your side, but his sole allegiance is the Divine. He will say and do anything to advance that delusional cause. You would do well to disavow his counsel."

"And perhaps listen to you in his stead?" Tezcatlipoca replied, in a tone as dry as dragon breath. "This is not the first time you have offered me such advice. But who knows? Perhaps this time I will heed it. Perhaps you will bear that in mind the next time I call."

With that, he hung up. Drogo stared at his phone's blackened screen for a long moment, grudgingly impressed by the Great One's sly, backhanded bait. He liked that the old drake still had a little play left in him. That was going to make his downfall that much more delicious. He stuffed the phone in his breast pocket, then pulled out a cigarette and lit it.

"Enough planning for now, Aziz!" he said, wreathing the words in smoke. "Let's go and have ourselves a hunt!"

CHAPTER 4

Naga lounged semi-coiled in a sea of outsized cushions—a pose that might have seemed casual if not for the intensity of her unblinking stare. The object of her scrutiny was perched on a greasy wooden stool that Lee had dragged in from the kitchen. Her shoulders were slumped; her face, slack. Her eyelids were puffy from crying.

"*She looks broken,*" Naga remarked to her Chosen.

"*She lost home and dragon this night,*" Lee replied from the kitchen, deadpan as usual. "*How do you suppose she should look?*"

The response struck Naga as impertinent so she ignored it. "*She has been compromised. We should be rid of her before she compromises us, too.*"

"*How is she a threat?*" Lee wondered. "*The rest of the world thinks she is dead.*"

"*Illusions are temporary by nature. A single action, accidental or otherwise, can bring it crashing down.*" She paused to savor the hot, greasy smells that were spilling into the room and then added, "*I would pinch the bud off before it has a chance to flower.*"

Lee poked her head into the room and clucked at Naga like a disapproving hen. "*Food is almost ready,*" she said. "*You should make no decisions before you have eaten.*"

Naga arched her neck into a question mark. "*Why do you say that?*"

"*You are prone to hastiness when you are hungry,*" Lee replied, and then ducked back into the kitchen.

Naga heartily disagreed with that assessment, but to deny it outright when she was in fact ravenous after the night's goings-on would only make Lee think that she was right. *"Why should you care if I am hasty or not?"* she argued instead. *"You have no fondness for this woman. You denounced her as stubborn and close-minded after your first meeting. You were appalled that she had disregarded a drakena's Call for decades."*

"All true," Lee said. *"Before the end, however, she and the Great One did in fact bond. A degree of respect for that connection is due."*

As if Naga needed to be reminded of such things! As if she were not the older, wiser, more experienced member of this relationship! Sometimes, her Chosen could be downright presumptuous. Before Naga could shape her affront into a reproach, though, a surprisingly sardonic voice distracted her.

"So, what's the deal, dragon? Am I supposed to sit here all night?"

The outburst both intrigued and vexed Naga. Could Lee be right? Was Naga rushing to misjudgment here? Naga did not often entertain self-doubt but a wrong decision now could prove catastrophic for the next age so she thrust her great horned head into the woman's air space and snuffled her for insights. She reeked of stale fear sweat and strange chemical residues that first buzzed Naga's nostrils and then made her sneeze. The woman finger-combed a glob of dragon snot out of her hair and said something that Naga did not quite understand. Naga relayed what she had heard to Lee. *"What does 'airbag propellant' mean? Is it an insult?"*

"Not at all," Lee pulsed back, a reply tinged with distracted amusement. *"It's a kind of man magic that happens when a car crashes."*

Mollified, Naga resumed her study of the woman. Such a contradiction she was: both resigned and feisty, submissive but only just barely. Naga could smell the courage in her—and the grief. It was clear that curtailed or not, her bond with Quetzalcoatl had been deep and true. The compromise, wherever it had come from, had not originated there. Some outside agent had precipitated it then, an association that Naga could not sniff out try as she might. In a way, that made the woman an even more dangerous cypher.

"Is it just me?" she said then. "Or is this getting a little weird for you, too?"

There it was again, that pointed tone, sharp enough to prick a drakena's curiosity. Naga did not appreciate the jab. She wanted an easy resolution to this situation. She wanted the right answers here and now. Curiosity complicated matters. Yet here she was, on the verge of spitting up a worry pearl from wondering things about this woman. Had she invited compromise or had it found her of its own accord? Would the scars from her loss solidify her loyalties—or cause them to flow in some other direction? Had her daughter been tainted as well?

"Alrighty then," the woman said. "I guess that answers that."

At the same moment, the kitchen's double doors burst open with a violent bang and Lee came striding into the den with a cart heaped with steaming, spicy-smelling food. Quicker than a thought, Naga snapped out of the woman's air-space and into a slavering semi-coil. As soon as the cart stopped in front of her, she began gobbling down noodles like guts. Lee started back to the kitchen only to glide to a stop when the woman coughed a dry, shallow eh-eh into her palm.

"I'm a little dehydrated from all of the excitement," she said. "Could I have a glass of water?"

The request repulsed Naga. *"Water?"* she echoed, as she crunched a rack of barbecued pork into splinters. *"River dragons fuck in that stuff. Bring her plum wine."*

Lee was off and back in a heartbeat. "You should be grateful," she murmured, as she handed the woman an antique crystal goblet. "Naga rarely shares."

"Thank you," she said, raising the glass in Naga's direction.

"After the night I've had, a glass of wine is just what—"

"Do not speak to her while she's feeding," Lee scolded. "Discourse at such times is uncivilized."

"But—you said I should be grateful!"

When Lee shrugged, refusing to argue the point, the woman scourged her with a look and then guzzled her wine dragon-style. "Just so we're clear," she said, as she set the empty glass down, "it's not the discourse going on in this room that's uncivilized."

Naga snorted, spraying a fair number of pillows with flecks of half-masticated flesh in the process. Now that she had a little food in her belly, she could better appreciate the woman's wit. She pulsed a thought at Lee: *"Give her another."*

Lee went to refill the woman's glass only to be waved off. "Thanks," she said, "but a second one would knock me on my ass. I'm so tired, I'm shaking. I'm achy all over, too."

"You were in a car wreck," Lee remarked flatly. "Some soreness is to be expected. Your advanced age is probably a contributing factor as well."

The woman reared back, projecting indignation. "Do you have to work at being rude? Or were you born that way?"

Lee's eyes narrowed. The muscles in her neck and jaws tensed. "How I was born is none of your concern, *barang.*" Then, with a toss of her head, she sauntered back into the kitchen like an affronted cat. The woman saw Lee off with a sour face and then turned that scowl on Naga.

"Now what?"

The cart was empty except for the few meager scraps that were beneath a dragon's notice. Naga scoured her muzzle with her coarse, contortionistic tongue and then focused on the woman again. Nothing had changed. She was still cryptic. Naga still needed answers. Unfortunately, the food in Naga's belly was making Naga lazy. Naga did not want to interrogate the woman. Naga wanted to spend the rest of the night in the comfort of her native form.

"*Come back here,*" she pulsed to Lee. "*We must interview this woman.*"

Lee's response flew out of the kitchen like a steel-tipped arrow. "No! I am busy. Ask your questions yourself."

The woman cocked her head in Naga's direction. "What is it that you want to know?"

Her tone sounded genuine enough, but it wasn't what Naga wanted to hear. Naga wanted to hear Lee asking the questions. She withdrew from the link for a few minutes and then, trying to seem patient, polite even, made contact again. "*Are you unbusy yet?*" When Lee ignored her, Naga heaved a reproachful harumph and grudgingly began to reshape herself.

The Change did not come without pain, a sensation that Naga made no effort to keep private. Naga groaned as her body shifted. Naga growled as her bones shrank. Afterward, as Naga wrapped her soft bare self in one of the silk robes that she kept stashed in her nest, she fixed the woman with a dragonish glower and croaked, "You had better be worth this."

For her part, the woman seemed unfazed by what she had just witnessed and possibly even slightly amused by Naga's show of distemper. Her lack of awe irritated Naga. "Do you— laugh at me?"

"Hardly," the woman replied. "More like I know how you feel—me being of an advanced age and all."

"Ah," Naga said, mollified by the ironic slant to her tone. "I understand now. You meant to commiserate. How quaint."

The woman flinched ever so slightly, then went completely straight-faced. "So, what can I do for you, dragon?" she asked.

From the kitchen, Lee shouted, "Her name is Naga!"

"And mine is Aurora," the woman said, "since we're sharing.

But I have a feeling that that's not what you want to know."

A second prompting. Interesting. Was this earnestness on her part or a dodge in disguise? Naga picked a bit of bone from her teeth with a long, thick pinky-nail as if she were digging for insights. Finding none, she decided to be uncharacteristically direct. "I need to decide what to do with you."

Aurora scowled as if she sensed something amiss with the statement but could not give the impropriety a name. "Thanks," she said, trying to sound earnest rather than puzzled, "but you've done more than enough already. I can do for myself from here."

Naga denied the claim with a shake of her head. "You have been compromised."

Aurora's scowl deepened: instinct scratching at the door. "You don't know that."

"On the contrary," Naga countered. "The Great One is dead. Tonight. You were almost killed. Tonight. At the end of an age, there are no coincidences."

The color drained from Aurora's cheeks. The corners of her mouth grew heavy. Naga understood immediately that she had provoked more than acceptance from the woman. "You grieve for the Great One."

"Yes," Aurora admitted, eyes downcast.

"What does such a loss feel like?" Naga asked, "I have never known the like."

"It's hard to describe," she replied. "When my husband died, I felt abandoned and adrift, like I'd been stranded on a too-small raft in the middle of the ocean. With Quetzalcoatl, I feel—diminished. The place in the back of my mind where we were joined feels like a bombed-out bridge." She gnawed on her lower lip for a moment and then added, "The weird thing is, I'm getting these fuzzy-wuzzy flashes that kind of feel like she's trying to reestablish contact with me. Is that possible? Are there ghost dragons?"

"No," Naga said. "When dragons die, their bodies turn to ash and their essences reunite with the Divine."

Aurora relinquished that hope with a sigh and said, "I guess I must be suffering from phantom limb syndrome."

"What is that?"

"People who lose a limb often complain that they can still feel pain in the amputated part. Apparently, the pain can be quite intense."

"Ridiculous," Naga said. "Flesh dies when it is separated from the body. Death is the cessation of sensation."

"The sensations aren't coming from the missing parts," Aurora said. "The amputee's body is creating them."

Ah, now that made more sense to Naga. When Naga was in human form, she could still feel her tail sometimes. There was no pain involved, but Naga supposed that there could be if she hurt her tail prior to Changing. She started to contemplate an experiment only to be distracted by another eh-eh from Aurora.

"Actually, there is one more thing that you can do for me," she said, looking suddenly more anxious than sad. "In all the excitement, I forgot all about my daughter. She'll be worried sick if she saw the late-night news. Can you lend me a phone so I can call her?"

Naga, too, had forgotten about Aurora's daughter but she wasn't about to admit that out loud. Instead, she said, "We know Roz-a-lyn. She has a dragon's heart. Where is she?"

"I don't know," Aurora said, trying to contain her distress. "She and her drakena set out to—"

"Wait." Now it was Naga's turn to struggle for composure. The daughter had bonded with a drakena—while the mother was alive? Incredible! Unprecedented! And outrageous that

Naga was only hearing about it now! "You say Roz-a-lyn has bonded? When did this happen? When last we spoke, only the potential existed."

"She met Brigit while she was visiting Loch Ness," Aurora said. "Apparently, the drakena had been Calling her for some time."

"I see. And how is that that two different drakena Called to two different women in the same family?" Naga asked, both intrigued and inexplicably suspicious.

"Rosalyn's father was of Scottish descent," Aurora said. "Brigit hails from that side of her heritage. My ancestors were Mayan, who were Quetzalcoatl's Chosen people."

"I suppose such an outcome had to happen eventually in this age of global travel and mixing of cultures," Naga mused aloud. "Even so, this is remarkable, a sign from the Divine. Where is your daughter now? I would speak with her."

"I don't know," Aurora said, projecting irritation now as well as anxiety. "The last I heard, she and her drakena were heading south to check out a bit of information that they got from the wyrm they saved—"

"Wait. They saved—a wyrm?" Naga echoed, appalled by the extent of her own ignorance. "How is that possible?"

Aurora's expression shifted from a weary blank to something craftier. "Lend me a phone and I'll tell you everything I know."

Naga smiled, a thin-lipped bend of the mouth that could've been construed as menace. "You dare to bargain with a dragon?"

Aurora dismissed the potential threat with a shrug. "I'm desperate," she admitted. "Roz has probably heard about the fire by now, and maybe the car crash, too. I need to let her know I'm OK."

"I cannot let you make that call," Naga said.

"Why?" Aurora asked—a note of pure protest. "Roz will be out of her mind with grief and worry!"

"We do not know the nature or the extent of your compromise," Naga said, deflecting Aurora's distress with calm. "A call from you might expose her—or us. Our lives—and our purpose—is more important than her heart's ease."

"Then let me call my friends instead," Aurora said. "They can contact her for me. They could probably come and pick me up, too."

Naga considered the proposal for a moment and then offered conditions. "There is a payphone in the store," she said. "When I open for business tomorrow morning, you may make one phone call so long as is it not to your daughter. In return, you will tell me everything I want to know."

"Tomorrow?" Aurora echoed, a sound like a heart breaking. "But—"

Naga forestalled her with an upraised forefinger. "The shop is warded. I will not disturb the warding for a call that can be made in the morning."

"But—"

"No," Naga said, a refusal as solid as a closing door. "I have lived here undetected for over a century because I do not do things that might draw attention to myself. You would be wise to start learning to do the same."

"But—"

"You have my word: you will have your call. Tomorrow."

Aurora hung her head, acknowledging defeat. "All right then. Beggars can't be choosers, I guess."

"No, they cannot," Naga said. "And while you are waiting for morning to come, you should fulfill your end of the deal."

"Fine," Aurora said tersely. "Tell me what you want to know."

Now that the negotiations were over, Naga settled deeper into her cushions, readying herself to listen. As an afterthought, she called to Lee to bring her the little smoke.

"I am not your servant!" Lee shouted, even as she went to

fetch the hookah.

"What's her problem?" Aurora asked, quick to revive her grudge.

"Lee's life has not been easy," Naga said, feeling no need to guard her Chosen's secrets. "The Divine placed her in the wrong body."

"What?"

"Lee was born female with male parts," Naga said, picking at her teeth again. "That would have been a confounding dissonance under any circumstance, but Lee had the added challenge of being foreign and poor in a land that has no tolerance for either condition. Had I not found her when I did, she probably would have died."

"I would have been just fine," Lee said, as she strode into the den with the hookah. She handed a hose to Naga and then lit a half-charred nob of opium in the bowl with a lighter. A thin curl of smoke rose up from the bowl: Naga's cue to draw on her stem. The first sip loosened her muscles. The second loosened her tongue.

"How old were you when I caught you in my shop helping yourself to my goods?" she asked Lee.

In lieu of a reply, Lee sat down next to Naga and took a puff from Naga's stem. The smoke smoothed some of the toughness from her face and made her seem softer than she was. Naga caressed her Chosen's long, black hair and said, "You were eleven, I think. Or maybe twelve. Bold as brass even then."

"Did you know she was that young when you Called her?" Aurora asked.

"Ah," Naga said, "but I did not Call her. I was of a mind that her bloodline had died out."

Aurora leaned forward on her stool, a subconscious shift toward the storyteller that those who loved stories often made. "Why did you think that?"

Naga smiled, then took another pull from the hookah and said, "To know the present, you must look into the past."

Lee shot Aurora a reproachful look and said, "Now you've done it."

But Naga was pleasantly stoned and did not take offense.

"My dam was Huanglong the Yellow," she said, "She who brought the elements of writing to the Emperor Fu Shi. My sire was a nameless fire drake from the north. I came to awareness in the Sacred Mountains of southeastern China at the start of the fourth age. My dam called me and my clutch-mates an accident—you know what I mean by this?"

Aurora nodded, a slow bob, as if she were catching a contact high.

"It was a time of great upheaval for Huanglong. Men and drakes were feuding. Drakena were no longer welcome at court. Had she been alone, she might have been able to persuade the emperor to grant her sanctuary on one of his estates. But not even an emperor would have risked harboring her and a clutch of newly sexed dragons. She could have left us on our own to go wild. Instead, despite her dismay at our existence, she took us deep into the mountains and taught us how to be proper dragons.

"Or at least she tried.

"The new age was still in its infancy when I wearied of her lessons. Astrology bored me. Making rain seemed pointless. And really, how many warding spells does anyone need to know? Huanglong grew weary of my contrariness and dismissed me. I did not care. I was young and life was new and I wanted to learn things for myself. I wandered from mountaintop to mountaintop, reveling in experiences. Rivers talked to me. Flowers told me their names. I discovered a thousand new smells.

"Then, one summer morning, just before dawn, I met my first human.

"She was standing on the banks of a watery field, directing a swarm of other, smaller humans with baskets to different parts of the paddy. A creature of some power, I surmised, and decided to investigate. As I emerged from the jungle, the smaller beings shrieked and started to run. The other, in contrast, calmly stood her ground and watched as I advanced. That excited me. How fearless was she? I stomped. I snorted. She met my gaze without flinching until I was less than a grand dragon's length away. Then she pointed at the ground in front of me and made two noises.

"'Tiger trap'.

"I did not understand the sounds at the time, but her gesture guided my eyes to a patch of thatch and debris between us. As I stared at it, trying to make sense of its existence, the human tossed a small boulder into its center. The patch collapsed, exposing a pit filled with stakes that were long enough and sharp enough to pierce a young dragon's hide. I realized then that the human had saved my life. Honor demanded that I repay her.

"So it was that she became my first Chosen.

"Her name was Zhi, and at the time of our first meeting, she had little understanding of anything except the life cycle of rice. I taught her how to write and make music and keep track of things with numbers. I also kept her warm at night, and watched over her as she and her younger clutch-mates worked in the fields during the day. She was a pleasant enough companion, so our connection was never strained, yet it lacked the kind of urgency that a young dragon craves. So, when she discovered love with the son of a trader who was moving his family to Cambodia to start a new life, I coughed up a dozen lucky pearls for her dowry and sent her on her way with a promise that I would find her or her daughters if they had need."

"Seems fair enough to me," Aurora said, but Naga could not tell if she was being earnest or not. "Where did you go?"

"A rumor of easy wealth lured me to the new world," Naga said, suffering a nostalgic pang. "I discovered gold country first, and then San Francisco. I claimed the city as my territory and had many, many fine adventures. Then, a century and a half later, another rumor caught my attention. This one came with a name: Pol Pot."

"'To keep you is no benefit,'" Aurora murmured. "'To destroy you is no loss.'"

Naga nodded grimly. "I see you are familiar with the snake."

"Only in passing," Aurora said, still half-lost in whatever memory the name had conjured. "He was one truly evil human being."

"Do you know nothing?" Lee warbled, opium-amused. "Pol Pot was no human."

Aurora gaped at her for a moment, obviously debating whether Lee was to be believed or not. Then, still undecided, she looked to Naga for confirmation. "Pol Pot was a drake?"

Naga responded with another grim nod. "I did not recognize him for what he was when the rumors about him first started swirling, for there has never been a shortage of men who live to commit atrocities against their own kind. Then one day the full scope of his malice broke out on the news: over a million dead in the killing fields of Cambodia. My thoughts turned to Zhi's descendants. They were of Chinese descent, and merchant stock as well—a favored target of his Khmer Rouge. I reached out through my bond. I reached for a long, long time. When I finally made contact, the first sensation that greeted me was cold, dark terror."

She took another sip of smoke to dull the memory. "Next, I sensed pressure: face, chest, legs, and belly being weighed down by a steady barrage of hard, damp clods and stones."

Aurora's hands flew to her mouth, a heartbeat too late to hide the mixture of recognition and horror that blossomed there. "My God," she said, breathing the words past her fingers. "She was being buried alive!"

"So I assume," Naga said.

"How did she escape?"

"She did not," Naga replied. "I know because we were still linked when she drew her last dirt-clogged breath."

"Oh," Aurora said, and then lowered her eyes, a moment of silence for the unnamed dead. When she looked up again, her brow was ridged with afterthoughts. "But if she didn't escape—" She glanced at Lee. "How did you get here?"

In response, Lee unfurled herself, rising to her feet with the grace of a lily in bloom. Her features were still soft, but the guarded glint was back in her eyes. "As I said before," she said, as she strode past Aurora, "my history is none of your concern."

To Naga, she said, "I will sleep now. Do not disturb me until you decide what you are going to do with her."

Aurora narrowed her eyes at Lee's retreating back and then turned that look on Naga. "So, what are you going to 'do' with me?

"You have no home and no dragon," Naga said, feeling less garrulous now that the little smoke was leaving her body. "You cannot stay here because the drakes know who you are. For the same reason, I should not let you go. So, you tell me: what option does that leave?"

Understanding splashed across Aurora's face, followed by surprise and disbelief. "Would you really kill me—after all the trouble you went through to save me?"

"It does seem wasteful," Naga acknowledged, and then went dragon-sly. "Maybe another solution will come to me while you're telling me about that wyrm."

CHAPTER 5

A terrible buzzing sound roused Roz from a sweaty, fractured sleep. She flopped onto her back and then gasped like a landed fish as pain ignited in her head. Her throat felt like three days in the desert; her eyeballs felt parched as well. Her sole desire was flop back onto her belly and burrow into the knotted, bourbon-scented sheets. But even as she gave herself permission to do so, a low rumble drifted up from the floor.

"Shut tha feckin' thing up."

"'Tha thing' was her cell phone, which was stuffed into the back pocket of the jeans that she had neglected to peel off before falling into bed last night. She dragged the phone forth and then squinted at its face, trying to puzzle out why Mara would be calling so early in the morning. Something terrible must have happened. A moment later, she remembered what that terrible something was and scrambled to answer the call before it went to message.

"Mar?" she said, wincing at the sound of her own voice. "What's up? Any news?"

"She's alive!" Mara sang in reply.

"Wait." Her brain wasn't working. She couldn't have possibly heard that right. "What?"

"Your mother's alive, Rosalyn!" Mara said, an even louder and higher-pitched song.

Last night, Roz had refused to accept the news about Aurora. Now that she didn't need that shield of denial, she couldn't seem to put it down. "How do you know?"

"I just got off the phone with her," Mara said. "We're going to pick her up."

Euphoria crashed over her—that glorious sense of gratitude and relief that came with an answered prayer. Then, as the significance of Mara's claim sunk in, her joy broke into a million shards of disbelief. "Wait," she said. "She called you? Instead of me?"

"She only had one phone call—"

"What? Is she in jail?" Damn, it hurt to think. Her brains felt like they were sloshing against the inner walls of her skull. "What did she do?" The sloshing churned up a feasible possibility. "Is she covering for Quetzalcoatl? Did that dragon kill someone?"

The connection went silent for a moment: Mara figuring out what she wanted to say next. "The Great One is dead," she said. "A drake killed her. Drakes tried to kill your mom, too— and damn near succeeded. She didn't want to tell us any of this at first because she didn't know we knew about Quetzalcoatl, but once we convinced her that we were in on the secret, she filled us in on everything."

Roz sputtered, thinking, 'But!' and then stalled. There was a blockage in her thought processes. None of this shit made sense. "But why didn't she call me?" she bleated. "I'm her daughter!"

"Are you OK?" Mara asked, and Roz could almost see the concerned furrow that had taken possession of her forehead. "You sound a little—off."

Roz's first impulse was to deny the observation. On second thought, she decided that she was incapable of anything other than the naked truth. "Of course I sound a little off," she said. "I spent the better part of last night trying to counteract reality with bourbon."

"Oh," Mara said, a crinkly-nose mix of sympathy and disapproval. "Do you really need to adopt all of that dragon's bad habits?"

"Hear that?" Roz said, an over the shoulder query. "Mara thinks you're a bad influence."

Brigit's only response was a sleepy grunt.

"No comment from the dragon," Roz said. "So, back to my question. Why did my mother call you instead of me?"

"Well, for one thing, whoever compromised her probably knows about you, too," Mara said. "Which means that you might be being hunted, too. She didn't want to risk exposing you by calling."

The possibility of her being in danger didn't faze Roz in the least. She was fixated on the phone call that she didn't get. Her mother would have known that the news of her death would devastate her daughter. And she wasn't the sort of woman who would let a loved one suffer like that, risks notwithstanding.

"What's the second thing?" she asked.

"Excuse me?" Mara said.

"You said 'for one thing'. That must mean there's another. What is it?"

Mara cleared her throat, an uncomfortable little ahem, and then said, "The drakena who rescued your mother kept her confined overnight."

Shit! Another dragon? Her alcohol-ravaged brain couldn't handle another twist! Why did things have to be so fecking complicated? "Which drakena is this?"

"Her name's Naga."

The name rang a loud bell which then dislodged a memory rooted in Chinatown. "That bitch!" she said. "I should have known."

A pause ensued—a moment of surprise mixed with wonder. "You know her?"

"Yeah," Roz said. "You do, too. Leastwise you'd recognize her if you saw her." Part of her wanted to dwell on her spanking-new grudge, but her practical side prevailed. "So, what's the plan? You taking Mom back to your place?"

"Negative," Mara said. "Everyone thinks she's dead so we're heading somewhere more remote to perpetuate that perception."

"Where exactly?"

"Her cottage on the lake," Mara said. "Max and I are going to stay with her."

Her friend's generous spirit made Roz's heart ache with gratitude. She wanted to tell her that such a sacrifice wasn't necessary, that her mother was safe now that Quetzalcoatl was dead, but she knew 'safe' wasn't the only consideration involved here. Aurora would surely be fragile after suffering the loss of both home and dragon. She'd fare better with company to look after her.

"Thank you so much, Mar. You and Max are the best," she said instead. "I'm sorry you got dragged into this mess."

"Hey, she's our mom, too," Mara replied. "And to tell the truth, we're kind of excited to be involved. It's an adventure."

Roz scowled only to regret the movement a microsecond later. And damn! Why did her mouth taste so bad? "Yeah well," she said, "with any luck, this part of the adventure is over."

"Yeah well," Mara fired back, "I'm not so sure about that."

Rather than Mara's spidey-sense, Roz changed the subject. "When do you expect to arrive at the cottage?"

"We'll be making pitstops along the way," Mara said, "so later tonight."

"My axle should be good to go sometime this morning," Roz said. "That puts us at the lake midday tomorrow."

That provoked another apprehensive ahem.

"What?" Roz asked, with more snap in her tone than she'd intended.

"You have to stop in San Francisco first," Mara blurted, well aware of how Roz would react to the 'have-to'. "Naga has invited you and Brigit to visit."

"Fuck her," Roz fired back, and then winced as the burst of outrage jarred the pulsating glob of mush that used to be her

44

brain. "After the hell she put me through last night, I'm never going within fifty miles of Chinatown."

"If you don't accept her invitation," Mara continued, "she won't let Aurora go. It's a condition of her release."

Roz's outrage blistered like an aneurysm, threatening to give her a stroke. She ground her teeth against the urge to shout and very softly said, "Unbe-fucking-lievable. She's using my own mother to manipulate me."

From her makeshift nest on the floor, Brigit said, "A say we go. If she invited us, she has ta feed us. And ye know how much A like Chinese food."

The buffet that the drakena had decimated back in their train-traveling days came to mind along with a vindictive thought: if nothing else, they could inflict that much damage on their would-be hostess. "OK, fine," she said grudgingly. "Tell Naga that we'll meet her at her shop sometime tomorrow. If she tries to hold on to Mom anyway, call me."

A muffled voice in the background intruded then. "What's that, love?" Mara asked, a hand over the phone question. A moment later, she was back to Roz. "Max says to dump your phone after this call."

"What?" Roz squawked. "No way! I paid two hundred bucks for this thing. Why on earth would I want to dump it?"

"Remember what I said about your mom being compromised?" Mara said, slipping into a conspiratorial half-whisper. "We don't know how extensive the compromise was, but it's not beyond the realm of possibility that she was being tracked her through her cell phone. Who's to say that your number hasn't been tagged, too?"

Roz rolled her eyes, not buying the theory. In a semi-snotty tone, she said, "Does this mean that you and Max are getting rid of your phones, too?"

Mara laughed, a curative sound. "Don't be silly! Nobody's looking for us. Wait, what's that, Max? Oh, OK." To Roz, she said, "I gotta jam, hon. It's time to load the car. See you soon! Love you, bye!"

Roz stared at the phone for a moment, thinking how lucky she was to have such awesome friends. Then, just as the screen was starting to fade to black, she noticed that she had voicemail. She must have slept right through the call—no, make that calls, seven in all, and all of them from Aldo.

"Hey, Roz. Where are you? We gotta talk. Call me!"

"Roz, did you hear the news? I don't wanna say what it is in a message. Call me!"

"Roz! I'm so sorry to be the bearer of bad news, but your house burned down! Call me!"

"Roz! Even if you're not speaking to me, call me to let me know you're OK! OK?"

She deleted the rest of the messages without listening to them. That fake concern wasn't fooling her. He'd gone from asshole ex-boyfriend to full-on stalker. All of a sudden, the idea of being tracked through her phone didn't seem so very far-fetched.

"Damn it," she said, as she threw the phone to the ground. "I should've let you eat him."

"Next time," Brigit promised.

CHAPTER 6

Charles stuffed bottle after bottle of vodka into the liquor cabinet, absurdly thinking, 'She loves me, she loves me not,' as he worked. The last one in was a 'loves me not'. That should've made him happy, but it pissed him off instead. Fucking new age. Fucking dragons. Fucking—

"Dude, OK if I fry up one of these mondo steaks? I'm starving."

Fucking moron.

"That meat is for Grishka Rasputin," Charles said, as he shut the cabinet door. "And in case you haven't noticed yet, dragons only share what's yours, never theirs. You take from him, you're likely to regret it."

Aldo ran a hand over his thinning hair and then looked nervously over his shoulder in the direction of the swimming pool. "Is he going to be staying here long?" he asked, in a near whisper. "He gives me the creeps."

Charles sneered. "He's a dragon, moron. He's supposed to give you the creeps. Now get your nose out of my fridge and tell me what you learned while I was out getting groceries."

"OK," Aldo said glumly, and then fished a folded piece of paper from the back pocket of his grungy jeans. "The cops were pretty close-mouthed about Aurora's accident. All they would say was that her car burned super-hot and that it will take weeks to extract her remains—if there are any."

She had to have been dead before the car exploded, Charles told himself. Had to. It was the only possibility that he could allow himself to imagine. "Do they know if the daughter was in the car with her?"

47

"Cops can't say but I'm pretty sure she wasn't," Aldo replied, perking up like he always did when the subject of his ex-girlfriend cropped up. When Charles encouraged him to elaborate with a raised eyebrow, he added, "I called her a bunch of times over the last twelve hours and went to voice mail every time. When I tried Aurora's number, I got an announcement that the call could not be completed."

Charles gave him grudging kudos for that tidbit, but when push came to shove, it wasn't really all that helpful. "So," he said, "if the daughter isn't dead, then where is she?"

"Beats me, dude. She's not answering my calls. Neither are her friends."

Hard to believe, Charles jeered to himself, and then gave free rein to his bad mood. "Is that it? Is that all you have? Because if it is, then you're of no use to me and you can get the hell out."

"But—you said I could stay here," Aldo whined. "And I can't go back to my place. We left my car at Aurora's when we fled the scene. The cops will be looking to question me."

"Yes," Charles said, oozing indifference, "I imagine you would be a person of interest to them."

Aldo's face scrunched up like a colicky baby's only to go smooth and sly a moment later. "You don't want them to find me," he said. "I'm not good under pressure. I might accidentally mention your name."

"Are you out of your fucking mind?" Charles asked, in a tone that was both incredulous and sinister. "If you so much as think about me in another person's presence, I'll hunt you down and feed you to yonder dragon. In fact," he added, seizing Aldo by a biceps, "maybe we should pay the old boy a visit right now."

"Wait," Aldo said, as Charles began to muscle him toward Grishka's watery lair.

"I don't think so," Charles said. "Better safe than sorry."

"Wait, wait, wait," Aldo begged. "I have something else for you. I just thought of it."

"What is it?" Charles asked.

"An address."

It was a beautiful evening for a drive, mild and mostly clear except for the patches of marine layer that poured over the Santa Cruz Mountains in the usual places. Charles opened the Jaguar up on the highway and would have sped all the way to their destination if traffic had not picked up and slowed down right at the San Francisco County line. Mood spoiled, he let up on the gas and resigned himself to driving slowly like the rest of the sheep.

"Take the San Jose Avenue exit," Aldo instructed when the time came, and then for fifth or sixth time, remarked on how smoothly the car handled. "If you want to kick back after we're done here, I could drive back. I'm a great driver."

"No," Charles said, wishing he could've left the moron at home with the dragon. But he didn't know the city or the people he was looking for, so he was stuck for a guide. Aldo took him into an older neighborhood that boasted blocks of dowdy rowhouses intermingled with small businesses, Chinese take-out joints, and the occasional bar.

"There," he said, pointing at a gentrified apartment building at the top of the street. "That's the place. And we're in luck, there's a parking spot right out in front!" When Charles cruised right past it, he yelped, "Are you nuts? Parking spots are gold in this city. You see one, you grab it!"

"This isn't the kind of job you park out front for," Charles drawled, and went in search of a less conspicuous place to park. As luck would have it, one opened up just a block away.

"Want me to wait here?" Aldo asked, as Charles got out of the car. Charles resisted the urge to slap him. "You're the one who knows these people. You do know them, right?"

Aldo scoffed. "Absolutely. Roz used to drag me up here all the time to see them. They're on the third floor. But like I told you before, the building's got security."

"Buzzer system and surveillance cameras, right?" Charles said, as he popped the Jag's trunk. "But no front desk." He handed an empty pizza box to Aldo." This is for you. And this," he added, pulling out his murder bag, "is for me."

"What am I supposed to do with this?" Aldo asked, looking affronted.

"Carry it like there's a pizza inside," Charles said. "People trust people who are carrying pizza."

"Oh," Aldo said, and then struck a stylized box-over-the-head pose with the box. "Like this?"

"Must you always behave like a circus ape?" Charles snapped. "Just carry the fucking thing like a normal human being."

Aldo lowered the box, lapsing into a wrongly accused sulk along the way. "I can't help it if I'm naturally theatrical."

"You're going to be naturally dead if you draw undue attention to us," Charles said, a threat that was no less sincere for having been so casually made. "Now let's go. When we get to the front door, push buttons until someone buzzes you in. If anyone asks who you are, don't get 'theatrical', just say, 'Pizza delivery.'"

"Where are you going to be?"

"Right behind you," Charles said. "It would look suspicious if we were bunched up." Not to mention that he didn't want to be seen with his designated fall guy.

As it happened, they didn't even need the plan. A guy carrying a Pizza Hut warming bag was on his way out just as Aldo was bounding up the steps. He held the door open for his fellow delivery dude and then wished him a nice evening in passing. Aldo left the door open a crack for Charles and then headed for the elevator. Charles thought about redirecting him to the stairwell only to change his mind. There would be a security camera in the car. The footage would come in handy if things got messy.

"You go ahead," he said, when Aldo motioned for Charles to join him. "I'm taking the stairs."

"But it's three flights up!" Aldo said.

Charles shrugged and then disappeared into the stairwell. Three flights later, he emerged to find Aldo standing halfway up the hallway. "This is it," he whispered, as Charles closed in on him. "Three twelve. What now?"

"Knock," Charles said. "If they come to the door and ask what you're doing here, say you came because you can't get in touch with Roz and you're worried about her."

Aldo rapped at the door several times, but got no response. "They must be out," he said. "They go to the movies a lot."

By then, Charles was already picking the locks.

As soon as he eased the door open, he knew the Marinos weren't home. The air smelled of detergents. There were no dishes in the sink, no clothes in the hamper, no water droplets in the sinks or showers. Their bed was neatly made, but the bedroom closets looked like they had been ransacked.

"Packed in a hurry," Charles remarked, taking note of the discrepancy.

"Nothing much in the fridge, either," Aldo said, shuffling into the room with a mostly empty carton of Chunky Monkey ice cream in hand. "Guess they must be on vacation."

"I guess," Charles echoed, as he casually regarded the collection of framed pictures that studded the top of the antique dresser. "Go and check their land-line for messages."

An old photograph in a handmade, pink dragonshaped frame snagged his attention. It was of three grinning teenagers—and Aurora. She must have been in her thirties when the picture was taken. She was smiling for the camera, a slightly self-conscious bend of the lips that contrasted the joyful gleam in her eyes. His stomach clenched, a spasm of reflexive grief and yearning. Oh, how he wished he had known her then! He might have been able to keep her from falling in with the drakena. He could have taken her someplace safe. If he had reached her in time, she might still be alive today and they might still be together. He was so caught up in his wishful fantasy, he didn't realize that Aldo had returned until he cleared his throat. Then he reached over Charles' shoulder and tapped the tall, auburn-haired teenager in the picture.

"That's Roz," he said. "She was a hottie even as a kid. These two losers," he went on, pointing to the dark-haired duo to Roz's left, "are Max and Mara. I guess they must have popped out of the womb as geeks. And that's Aurora. But you probably already know that."

"Yes," Charles said, reluctantly returning to the real world. "I know that. Anything on the answering machine?"

"Nothing." He waited for a seemingly respectful moment and then said, "Now what?"

"You need to come up with another name or address," Charles said.

Aldo voiced his signature protest—a vociferous, "Dude!" He then went on to say, "I told you Roz wasn't all that social. She mainly hung out with these two or her mother."

Charles thrust one of the other photos at him. "Who're these people?"

"I don't know. Ozzie and Harriet maybe?"

Charles let the wisecrack pass for the moment and singled out another photo. "Who's this?"

"No clue, Magoo."

Charles grabbed a third frame. At the same time, he kicked his murder bag into Aldo's shin—almost by accident, it seemed. "Now," he said, injecting menace in his tone, "before you give me another smart-ass answer, I want you to think really hard about what's going to happen to you if you are no longer useful to me."

"Dude," Aldo said, raising his hands as if in surrender, "I've done everything you asked me to."

"Yes, you have. Now I'm asking you to tell me something about this photo." He shoved the frame under Aldo's nose, barely resisting an urge to mash it into his face. "Who is this? Where is this?"

Aldo's forehead was shiny now and his cheeks were flushed. "That's Max without a beard. Those dumpy old folks must be his—I dunno, grandparents?" Charles nudged his bag with a toe. The sheen on Aldo's brow blistered into a sweat. "I'm telling you, man, I don't—wait! Wait, wait, wait! That's Chinatown in the background. Roz and I were there the day she invited me to go to Scotland with her." He squeezed his eyes shut, trying to wring the memory into recall. "We were having lunch at the 'Empress of China.' Aurora was there, too. She and Roz were going on and on about some place they used to live. It was a cottage, I think—on a lake."

"What lake?" Charles said, softly so as not to rattle the moron out of his recollection.

"Shit!" Aldo said, scrunching his whole face up now. "What was the name of it? It's on the tip of my brain. 'Look, Mommy!', he said, in a childish falsetto. "'Dragon's breath!'" Then he snapped his fingers, opened his eyes, and said, "That's it, that's the name! Dragon's Breath Lake."

Charles blinked, caught totally off-guard. "Seriously? There's a place called that?"

"Well, that's what they called it. Its real name is something super-weird."

"And where is this lake located?" Charles asked, soft still but in an entirely different way.

"Up north somewhere," Aldo said, waving vaguely.

"Can you be more specific?"

"Not at the moment."

"That's too bad," Charles said, flipping the safety in his head to 'off'. "Because I've got deadlines to meet. If this is the best you can do, then we're done."

"Wait!" Aldo exclaimed, as Charles reached for his bag. "I didn't say I couldn't name the place. I just need a little help. Show me a map of northern California—or better yet, a list of all the lakes in northern California. As soon as I see the name, it will ring a bell. I swear."

Charles grumbled. The proposal had so little promise, it barely qualified as marginal. Nevertheless, next to nothing was better than nothing at all, and what choice did he have? As happy as he would have been to leave this moron's corpse here for the residents to find when they finally came home, he had to have a next move and apparently, this was it.

"If you're jerking me around," he said, "I'll make sure you're still alive when the dragon starts eating you."

"I'm not messing with you, dude," Aldo swore. "Just give me a chance. All I need is the right visual."

Charles grumbled again—a grudging stay of execution. Then he tucked the picture of Aurora and her daughter into the inner pocket of his jacket and gestured toward the door.

CHAPTER 7

The cottage smelled of trapped air and Pine-Sol: a tell-tale sign of disuse. Aurora did not appreciate the funk, but it certainly came as no surprise. Between her work schedule and Roz's lack of interest in bucolic lakeside getaways, it had been almost a decade since Aurora had spent any time here. Her tax advisor wanted her to get rid of the place, but part of her was still attached to it for sentimental, Duncan-related reasons. So, she hung on to it, offering it to friends or friends of friends who needed a vacation or just a change of scenery. Lord MorFang the Screamer and his brother had been here last, working on a musical entitled, 'It's Your Funeral'. That had been six months ago. Since then, the cottage had sat empty—an open invitation to spiders and mice. As she pulled the dust-cover from the living room couch, one of those four-legged pests went scurrying across the hardwood floor and into a gap between two baseboards. She eeked—an involuntary reaction. Mara did the same from the other side of the room.

"Everyone OK?" Max shouted, from one of the bedrooms.

"Yeah," Mara shouted back. "But we need to add mouse traps to the list."

Max strode into view, a dust rag slung over his shoulder like a burp cloth. "The beds are ready to be made up," he said. "I had a good look; they're both vermin-free."

"Excellent," Mara said, and then turned to Aurora. "Which room do you want?"

She flushed, abashed anew by her con-kids' willingness to put themselves significantly out for her. "Listen, you guys," she said. "I really and truly appreciate the thought, but you don't have to do this."

"Oh yes we do," Mara said. "You're supposed to be dead, so we can't have you being up here alone drawing attention to yourself. We'll be your cover: a couple from San Francisco here on vacation. Don't worry," she added, when Aurora continued to balk, "Max and I can both work remotely—not that I have any to speak of at the moment. And it's certainly no hardship hanging out by a beautiful lake with my all-time favorite writer friend."

Aurora swallowed hard, but her reservations refused to go down. She turned to Max, the more reasonable of the two, and tried again. "I can't access my bank accounts at the moment," she said. "This could wind up costing you a lot of money."

He deflected the argument with a shrug. "You'll get your life back eventually. On that happy day, you can pay us back. Keep a tab if you like. But like it or not, we are going to stay here until Roz turns up."

She wanted to protest again, but words failed her. In their stead, a sudden rush of tears welled in her eyes. She dropped the dust cover that she had been hugging to her chest and held out her arms. The next thing she knew, Max and Mara were both pressed against her, infusing her nose with their wholesome smells. "You are so precious to me," she said. "Thank you. I will find a way to repay you."

"First things first," ever-practical Max said. "Let's get this place squared away. What else do we have for the list?"

"Groceries," Mara said. "And wood for the fireplace. This time of year, it's going to get nippy at night."

"Let's go and get the food now," Max said, reaching for his car keys even as he spoke. "I don't want to wake up tomorrow and have nothing to eat."

"I'll finish tidying up here while you're gone," Aurora said, stripping him of his dust rag as he started for the front door.

As soon as the Marinos drove off, though, her energy bottomed out. She felt windblown and battered, shipwrecked on an island where Jabberwocks ran free and nothing else made sense. All she wanted to do was curl up in her favorite comfy chair and lose herself in a glass of wine. The chair was gone, though, burnt to the ground along with her house and the rest of her things... and Quetzalcoatl. In time, she could replace the things or at least most of them. But the drakena? How did one even begin to recover from a loss that fundamental?

Damn! She really wanted that glass of wine! There was none in the cottage, though, not even leftovers from the Screamer Brothers' extended stay. Hopefully, Mara had thought to put a few bottles on the list. Hopefully, she would remember that Aurora preferred reds—big reds with hints of cassis and dark chocolate and forest floor. The craving made her think of Charles. Was it mean of her to hope that he would be taking the news of her demise hard? An image of him took shape in her mind. He was standing next to the shed where they'd nearly made love, head bowed and arms folded across his chest. He wasn't praying, because he wasn't the sort who believed in prayer. Rather, he was trying to hold his grief in in the way that men did, blocking it out even as it broke over him. His face was stony; his mouth, a thin pale line that crooked downward at the corners. She imagined kissing some warmth back into that mouth. She imagined him knotting a hand in her hair. A complicated ache started to spread through her only to be arrested by a soft, scrabbly sound that seemed to be coming from the subflooring. Mice, she supposed, with a tiny shudder. Lots of them. Good thing Mara was picking up traps.

Now quit brooding and get to work!

She plodded into the nearest bedroom and began to make the bed that Max had prepped. The sheets were light pink—a faded hold-over from Roz's pre-teen obsession with Esmerelda. Aurora thought of Quetzalcoatl. How could she not? Part of her was sorry that she hadn't been home that night to defend the drakena against whatever it was that had taken her life. The rest of her was grateful that she hadn't been there. Otherwise, she would've surely been murdered, too. Did that make her a coward? Unworthy of a dragon's trust? She wrestled the fitted sheet into place as if it were her conscience and then froze as another round of scratching drifted into the room. This time, the sounds didn't bring mice to mind. This time, she got the distinct impression that someone was at the kitchen door, trying to get in.

"Max? Mara? Is that you?" she called.

The scratching came to an abrupt stop.

Shit.

She grabbed a long-necked ceramic vase from the dresser and went prowling back into the living area. A few days ago, she might have laughed at herself for being paranoid. Recent events, however, had completely reprogrammed her outlook. The vase was so old that it would probably shatter into a thousand pieces the instant she bashed it against the intruder's skull, but at least she'd get the first shot in and maybe buy herself a chance to bolt out the door, down the steps, and into the lake's wooded fringes. It wasn't much of a plan, but at least it was something.

The kitchen was dark save for the flimsy microwave light over the stovetop. She kept to the shadows, moving from wall to wall like a ninja in blue jeans. The entire cottage was quiet, as if it, too, was holding its breath. She snuck a peek at the kitchen door. The half-curtained window was like black ice, innocent-looking but fraught with hidden danger. All she could see in it was reflected glare. She crept closer, then closer still. The window continued to thwart her. She swore under her breath. Then, gathering her nerve into a fist, she flipped on the porch light and yanked the door open.

"Hai!" she shouted, as darkness fractured into light and shadows.

In response, a small, iridescent dragon with gossamer wings shouldered her aside and barged into the cottage. In passing, it hissed—a distinctly irritated sound. At the same time, a thought popped into her head.

"So slow you are! This one could have been seen!"

Shit! The weirdness was starting all over again!

This time, however, she wasn't caught entirely flat-footed. She closed the door, locked it, and turned out the porch light before turning to gape at her uninvited guest. Its face was long and narrow with a sloping forehead and large, quivering nostrils. Its eyes were kaleidoscopes. From the tip of its snout to the tip of its tail, it was no more than eight feet long. Every inch of it reeked of scorched earth.

"You're the wyrm everyone's looking for, aren't you?" she said.

"This one is wyrm no more," it replied, with a haughty huff. *"This one is Saidhe. You should know this."*

"How would I know a thing like that?"

Saidhe cocked her head, a look both quizzical and suspicious. *"We are bonded."*

Aurora started to laugh aloud at the absurdity of the declaration only to suck the breath back in as that psychic phantom pain impinged once again on her awareness. She had dismissed the feeling as her way of missing Quetzalcoatl, but now that the truth was staring in her the face, she realized that she was indeed engaged in an active link, albeit a young and undeveloped one.

"But—how?" she asked, shocked into stammering. "I was under the impression that bonding with a dragon was a singular thing."

"The Great One joined this one to you with her dying thought. She did not want either of us to be alone."

"You knew Quetzalcoatl?" Aurora asked, both excited by and envious of the prospect.

"We rode the Dreaming together," Saidhe said. *"This one took her to see the mountain where this one was reborn."*

"Then She sent Roz and Brigit off to see if they could find the place in real time," Aurora surmised. If She hadn't—well, Aurora just couldn't go there. Not today. Not ever. "I think I owe you a heap of thanks."

Saidhe rustled her wings and twitched the tip of her tail. *"This one does not know what 'thanks' might be. Do you have anything to eat?"*

"No," Aurora said, still trying to come to grips with the fact that this little drakena was now a flesh-and-blood part of her life. "We just got here. How did you find me, by the way?"

"We share a bond," Saidhe replied, projecting amazement at having to repeat something so basic. *"The bond brought me here."* She flared her nostrils then and inhaled deeply. *"There are mice in this place. Can this one eat them?"*

Dragons and their stomachs!

Saidhe must've interpreted the thought as permission to proceed, for she headed straight for the broken baseboard. Aurora was of a mind to let the drakena have her way simply because she wanted some time to process this turn of events, but even as she opened her mouth to say, "Have at," an afterthought derailed the plan.

"Wait!" she said. "Max and Mara will be back soon. They—"Don't know about you, she meant to say. But Saidhe cut her off with a thought frilled with approval.

"Yes. Max and Mara. This one knows them. They may stay."

"I'm sure they'll be happy to hear that," Aurora drawled. But what she was thinking was: when in hell had she become the designated last one to know? She flopped down on the couch, intending to sulk, but found herself watching Saidhe hunt instead. The drakena had settled into a crouch alongside the wall and was now snorting pillows of sulfur-tinged smoke into the crack—puff after patient puff until finally, suddenly, a family of mice burst out of the hole. Saidhe was on them in an instant, scooping the whole lot up with her lower jaw and then swallowing hard. A moment later, she disgorged a disappointed thought.

"That was not very satisfying."

"Sorry," Aurora said, although she feeling a little bit sorrier for the mice at the moment. Then, as Saidhe settled back into a crouch, another afterthought broke over her. "If you're going to stay here, you're going to have to look human."

"No," the drakena replied, punctuating the refusal with a puff of smoke.

"That wasn't a request," Aurora said, refusing to be shrugged off by a juvenile of any stripe.

"This one's human form does not look human," Saidhe said, a grudging explanation. *"It also resists this one's efforts to improve it."*

"Show me."

"Later, perhaps. When this one is finished hunting."

"Show me now," Aurora countered.

Saidhe launched a psychic glob of exasperation in Aurora's direction, then heaved a dramatic sigh and sat up on her haunches like a dog. An instant later, the air around her began to shimmer and thicken. A moment after that, the drakena disappeared within a three-dimensional distortion that was both beautiful and disturbing. Aurora blinked, trying to deflect a roiling sense of disorientation. The next thing she knew, she was looking at the spitting image of Francine the Woodland Fairy. She had iridescent skin, gossamer wings, and a hummingbird's ruby throat. Her ears were pointed; her eyes, almond-shaped. Aurora blinked again, a vain attempt to dispel her astonishment. Questions pelted her frontal lobe like a hard rain. How in hell could Quetzalcoatl have foreseen such a convoluted turn of events? And if She had, why had she not said anything to Aurora about it? Francine had never come up in their conversations, only in vague, early-on dreams. Did that mean that the Dreaming was behind this? To what point? And why her?

Damn. She wasn't in the right headspace to deal with this complication at the moment. The best she could do was lay down some ground-rules and hope for the best.

"OK," she said, "I can see how you might stick out in a crowd. But you can't hang out here in dragon form."

"This one is not hanging. This one is hunting."

With that, Saidhe reverted to dragon form and began plying the crack in the baseboard with smoke-signals again. A pang of warehoused maternal aggravation flared within Aurora— don't sass me, young lady! But before her pique had a chance to accelerate into a full-fledged burn, it fizzled, snuffed out by the sight of the drakena's whip-like tail twitching back and forth with predatory anticipation.

"Hey," she said, taken by a thought. "Do you know what a cat is?"

Saidhe rumbled, approximating a purr. *"Yes. They are very sleek and tasty."*

Not the two descriptors that Aurora would have strung together with a cat in mind, but the image that accompanied the thought was definitely feline. "Can you Change into one?" she asked.

"Possibly," Saidhe replied. *"This one has never tried."*

"Try now," Aurora urged. When the drakena ignored the request, preferring instead to maintain steadfast eye-contact with the mouse-hole, Aurora gave her a psychic flick and said, "The drakes are still hunting for you, little one. If you do not disguise yourself when you are hunting in human places, they will find you—and me, too. Then we'll both be screwed. So stop being a jerk and do as I tell you."

"This one does not recognize 'jerk'. Is it another sound for dragon?"

"Sometimes," Aurora said, starting to smolder again.

The drakena heaved another dramatic sigh and abandoned her watch on the crack. A moment later, she began to scintillate again. A heartbeat before the shimmer swallowed her up, she cast a sullen thought at Aurora. *"Just so you know, Changing is hungry work."*

A calico head emerged from the gyre first, then a muscular but streamlined body, and last of all, a long, thick tail. Saidhe-Cat stretched, elbows down and butt up, as if testing out the form. Her body was black with patches of iridescence. A pair of black nubs jutted up from the tops of her shoulder-blades. She looked to be the size of a young panther.

"Not bad," Aurora said, suitably impressed. "Not bad at all. Although it would help if you could lose the nubs."

The cat hissed, a very convincing feline reproach. *"Those are wing-buds. No matter what shape this one takes, they remain. This one does not know why."* Then, before Aurora could offer any further remarks, the changeling began circling after her tail—a curious, exploratory circuit. *"This one likes this form,'* she said. *"It feels most agreeable."*

Aurora watched, bemused. Bonding with Quetzalcoatl had been a difficult process, one hampered by a lifetime of pragmatic disbelief. Acceptance had come almost too late for her to appreciate the attachment on the level which it deserved.

Now, by The Great One's own doing, she found herself bonded to a second dragon! The situation struck her as surreal, laughable in its improbability. Yet even as she wrestled with incredulity, she felt something else stirring within her: the beginnings of gratitude for this second chance. This bond would not be the same as the one she had shared with Quetzalcoatl; she knew that already. But she'd worry about that later. For now, she was content to partake of the spectacle of a dragon-cat chasing her tail.

CHAPTER 8

It was a clear, warm afternoon in San Francisco—the perfect time for a trolley car ride through the city. Leastwise, according to Roz. Brigit didn't agree.

"Tha car's too crowded," she complained.

"Oh, come on," Roz cajoled. "That's part of the fun."

"Maybe fer ewe. A dunna like being around so many sweaty bodies. An' what's ta see? A bunch of buildings an' cars! Big feckin' deal!"

"Look!" Roz urged, as the trolley crested one of the city's highest hills. "You can see all the way down to the bay from here. Check out all the sailboats skimming across the water!"

Brigit responded with a noncommittal grunt. A few blocks later, she griped, "Tha air smells like salted dogshit."

"Too bad," Roz said, done with trying to jolly the drakena along. "We're doing this. If you don't like the ride, you can get off and walk. At the next stop," she hastened to add, before Brigit could vault from the still-moving trolley. "We're supposed to be keeping a low profile. Remember?"

"Feck that," Brigit grumbled. "Nobody's following us. A'da noticed by now."

"Hey," Roz said, throwing her hands up as if to ward off an attack, "I didn't make the rules. I'm just following them for Mom's sake."

The trolley bell rang, announcing the next stop. They disembarked and began walking toward Chinatown. "I dunna get it," Brigit said, scowling as she glanced this way and that. A person bumped into her. "Why would—?" Another person ricocheted off of her. "Why would any—?" A third person jounced her and then swore in a foreign tongue as he blended back into the foot traffic. "What tha feck?" she exclaimed. "A've had an easier time of swimming through a school of spawning salmon!"

"That's what you get for walking down the middle of the sidewalk," Roz said amicably. "Try keeping to the right like everybody else."

"But A'm not like everybody else," Brigit said, drawing herself up to her full height and girth. "A'm a fecking dragon."

"And a cantankerous one at that," Roz noted. "But please— go on with what you were saying. What don't you get?"

Brigit gestured widely, batting a passerby in the process. "Asshole," the woman snapped. "Same tae ewe," Brigit said, and then looked to Roz. "Why would a drakena choose tae live in such a filthy, foul-smelling place?"

Roz shrugged. "Different strokes, I guess."

"What's tha supposed ta mean?" Brigit asked, and then let out a glad shout. "There!" she exclaimed. "We're stopping there!"

"But—" Roz began, as the drakena made a beeline for the bar on the corner.

"No 'buts'," Brigit said, slinging the door open. "A'm not going any further until A've had a whiskey ta wash tha taste of this city outa my mouth."

The bar was a classic dive: small and dimly lit, with posters of hotties hawking beer on the walls and a dilapidated pool table in back. Although it was still early in the afternoon, there were no open seats at the counter. That didn't stop Brigit, though. She wedged herself into the space between two seats and then hip-checked the middle-aged man sitting to her right halfway off of his stool.

"Watch it," he grumbled, and then elbowed Brigit when she crowded him again. "I said, 'Watch it!'" When she twisted around to see what had bumped her, he added, "I was here first."

She eyed him with a mixture of slyness and contempt. "What will ye give me ta honor yer claim?"

"How about a fat lip if you don't?" he muttered into his half-empty beer mug.

"Are ye threatening me?" Brigit asked, managing to make a half-amused, half-wondering tone sound menacing.

He glanced up at her as if he were considering his next move, then grimaced and waved her away. "If I had wanted to get into it with somebody," he said, "I would've stayed home with my old lady. So why don't you be a peachie-poo and take your lady friend to the lesbo lounge down the street so I can drink my beer in peace."

Brigit pulsed a query at Roz. *"Lesbo lounge?"*

"Gay bar," Roz pulsed in reply. *"He thinks we're lovers."*

"Why?"

"I don't know," Roz said facetiously. *"Why don't you ask him?"*

Brigit did just that. "What makes ye think we're gay?"

The man came within a membrane of snorting beer out his nose. "You're kidding, right?" he asked, as he dragged a sleeve across his offended snout. "I mean, just look at the two of you! You're built like bulls! Hell, I'll bet your shit has muscles."

"Tha makes no sense," Brigit countered. "If shit had muscles, it would nae be shit!"

Another snort. Another near-beer aspiration. "It's a metaphor, for crap's sake," he said. "I'm just saying that you're big." He puffed out his chest to illustrate, then raised both arms like a prize-fighter and added, "Strong like bulls."

"Oh, stronger than tha," Brigit said, as she reached for the glass of straight-up whiskey that Roz had bought for her. "Much stronger. But what's tha connection between that and being gay?"

He must have mistaken her pernicious curiosity for passive-aggressive hostility because he lapsed back into truculence. "If you don't know," he said, "then I sure as hell ain't telling you. Now if you'll excuse me—" He drained the rest of his beer in a single defiant gulp, slammed the empty mug down on the bar, and then slid off his bar stool. "I've had just about enough of you."

Brigit watched the man exit the bar and then cocked her head at Roz. "Why wouldn't he tell me? Is it a secret?"

Roz smiled. "It's not a secret, dragon. It's bullshit. He's just a scared little man who demonizes people who are different from him to make himself feel superior."

"Truly?" She drained her own glass and then set it down. "Seems like a hard way tae live."

"Right?"

They started on their way again: down Powell, then over to Bush and on to Grant. "That's the ceremonial entryway into Chinatown," Roz said, pointing to the three ornate, green-capped portals that spanned across the avenue. "It's called The Dragon's Gate."

"Nice show of respect," Brigit said, nostrils flaring with approval. "Ye dunna see such things where A come from." As they passed through the nearer pedestrian portal, she stopped to look at the stone figure that seemed to be guarding the way. "Is tha what a Chinese dragon looks like? A've never seen one."

"Me, neither," Roz said. "But I know for a fact that that's a lion."

"Ah," Brigit said. "A've never seen one of those, either." A few steps later, she lifted her nose to the sky to better savor the smells of roasted duck and plum sauce that were oozing from a nearby restaurant. "Are we there yet?" she asked, licking back a fleck of drool. "A need tae feed soon. An' after that, A need tae spend some time in water. A'm getting a wee bit edgy, if ye know what A mean."

"I do know," Roz said, "and I'm sorry we had to make this detour. But Naga didn't leave me any choice. She said she'd kill Mom if we didn't show. I just couldn't take the chance."

"A know," Brigit said, and then lapsed into resigned silence. Roz hastened to tender a consolation prize. "If you want, we can head down to the wharf when we're done here. You could swim out to Alcatraz and snack on a shark or two. That might make you feel a little better."

The drakena sneered. "Have ye not smelled tha water? It reeks of cold, salt, and petrochemicals. Tha's not going ta make me feel better."

That shut Roz up, but only for a minute. If she didn't improve Brigit's disposition before they got to Naga's place, the drakena were likely to butt heads sooner rather than later, and Roz had absolutely no desire to find herself in the middle of that kind of cat-fight.

"We're just a few blocks away now," she said. "And man, am I hungry! When do you think she'll break out the grub?"

"She's a Loong," Brigit said gruffly. "A have no idea what kind of customs she keeps."

"It'll be interesting to see how another dragon lives," Roz said. "Don't you think?"

The drakena rumbled, projecting impatience. "With tha exception of Quetzalcoatl, A haven't interacted with another drakena since A left Ireland centuries ago—and A've been fine with that. A'd be surprised if it was different with Naga. We dragons like our space."

"Good to know," Roz said, thinking that she could use a little of that space herself right about now. Then The Empress of China spanned into view and she set her pique aside. "That's where it all started," she said. "I decided to go to Scotland while I was having lunch there. Afterward, I chased down a guy who stole my purse. He led me to Naga's back door and dragon tea—"

That snagged Brigit's attention. "Back doors are secret ways, heavily warded to repel the eye. If you saw hers, it was by her design. She showed you great favor."

"If you say so," Roz said, remembering that fetid back alley and Naga's unblinking stare. "At the time, it seemed more like an aggressive form of curiosity."

They were closing in on Naga's shop now. Roz recognized it by the bronze dragon that guarded the entryway. The sign on the door read, 'Closed'. She knocked anyway. As she waited for a response, she joined Brigit in admiring the sculpture. Had it really only been a few months since Mara had first called attention to it? Time didn't just fly; it had dragon wings! In spite of her prickly mood, the drakena seemed quite taken by the piece. She sniffed its chiseled scales as if they were real and then went to stroke its rounded muzzle. As she did so, the shop door swung open with a merry jingle.

"Can't you read?" a soft voice snapped. "The sign says, 'Don't Touch!'" Before either of them could respond, the voice went on. "Step inside. Quickly."

They complied. As soon as they cleared the threshold, a lean whip of a woman with long black hair locked the door behind them and then urged them toward the back of the shop. There, she addressed them directly for the first time.

"Were you followed?"

The woman had an oval face and delicate features. Her gaze was piercing. Roz peered at her for a moment, trying to resolve a niggling sense of recognition, and then blurted, "I know you!"

"I know you, too, Roz-a-lyn Vanderbilt," the woman replied frostily. "I ask again: were you followed?"

"Not a chance," Roz replied. "We left my truck at the airport and caught the BART to the Powell Street station. From there, we took a trolley to Bush and then walked through Chinatown. Nobody followed us."

The woman considered Roz's testimony for a haughty

moment and then looked to Brigit. "Is that your belief as well?"

"Ai, lass," Brigit said.

"Very well then," the woman said. "Come this way. Naga is waiting."

She led them through a secret door and down a broad, darkened hallway that smelled of hot oil and felt like it should not have been there. *"By the way,"* Roz pulsed to Brigit, as they followed along. *"That's no lass. That's the dude who stole my purse!"*

Brigit was quick to correct her. *"That one is not male."*

"But—I saw him! The part that counts, anyway."

"That's just plumbing. Look past that. Her identity is as female as yers."

"Yeah, but—" Roz said, finding the biology versus spirit hurdle too hard to clear.

Sensing her struggle, Brigit made an effort to tamp down her edginess and be patient. *"I dunna have a tail at tha moment. Does that make me any less of a dragon?"*

"No," Roz replied. *"But—you're a magical creature!"*

"We're all magical creatures, lass. Tha magic just comes easier for some of us." When Roz continued to balk, Brigit heaved a mental sigh and added, *"If ye cannot accept her for who she is, then ye can at least respect her right ta live her life according ta her own inner dictates. Otherwise, yer no different from that scared little man at tha bar."*

Roz blinked, stung by the comparison. She wanted to contradict the drakena, but found that she could not.

They came to a massive wooden door, a remnant from some long-forgotten era. Their guide turned to Brigit then, somber but respectful, and said, "Naga will receive you now. She will declare herself first. You will respond."

Brigit sighed, out loud this time, and the thought she then shared with Roz was the equivalent of an eye-roll. *"Feck! A hate ceremonies."*

Naga was seated on an ornate golden throne at the far end of the chamber, and while she was in her human form, the room's size and faint abattoir-like stench suggested that this was her dragon retreat. Her robes were black like her hair, and even from a distance, her eyes glistened like polished jade stones.

"Enter and be welcome," she said, motioning them to come closer with a frill of her dagger-tipped fingers. "I am Naga, daughter of Huanglong The Yellow, She who brought the elements of writing to the Emperor Fu Shi."

"Fancy," Brigit remarked to Roz, and then gave her fiery mane a haughty toss. "A am Brigit, She of the Sacred Flame an' the Hearth," she said. As a grudging afterthought, she added, "A'm known in some parts as tha Loch Ness Monster."

"Ah," Naga said, "a celebrity. How unfortunate." Then, looking past Brigit to Roz, she said, "Greetings, little one. Did I not say that there was more to you than you knew?"

"You did," Roz said, a flat admission. "You also said you weren't the enemy and yet you held my mother hostage and threatened her life. That doesn't seem very friendly to me."

Instead of taking umbrage, the drakena let out a horsy little laugh. "So fierce you are! So direct! But surely you know the difference between being unfriendly and being an enemy."

"Surely you know you're changing the subject," Roz fired back.

The drakena laughed again and then looked to Brigit. "You look depleted. Shall we feed before we enter into serious conversation?"

Roz felt Brigit's hunger rear up like a nest of starving snakes and readied herself to be put on indefinite hold. To her surprise, though, Brigit did not give in to that rapacious need. "A think ye need tae explain yer treatment of Aurora first."

Naga harumphed and threw her hands up in the air, a show of exasperation that may have been feigned. "Discourse before a feed is uncivilized," she said. "But since you have no aptitude for waiting, I will account for myself now.

"Your mother," she went on, addressing Roz again, "has been compromised. She cannot say how or when. The Great One died as a result of the breach. Everyone in this chamber could be in jeopardy as well. I do not know your mother, so I have no reason to trust her. Her only value to me is her value to you. If I had not threatened her life, would you have been so quick to accept my invitation?"

Everyone in the room had to know what the answer to that question was. But Roz wasn't going to give the drakena the satisfaction of a reply. Instead, she responded with a query of her own. "If we hadn't accepted the invitation, would you have followed through with your threat?"

Naga shrugged. "Who can say? I am not an oracle. But come now, I have answered your question, have I not? Can we not feed now? Hospitality fails me when I am hungry."

"Satisfied?" Brigit wondered—a thought awash with drool.

Although the answer to that was an emphatic, "Not by a lot", Roz didn't have the heart to deny the drakena sustenance any longer. "Yeah, have at it," she said. "I hope you don't mind if I don't stick around for the spectacle."

"As you wish," Naga said magnanimously. "Lee will see to your comfort."

"Go back the way you came," Naga's Chosen instructed her. "Find the kitchen. I will join you as soon as I am done here."

Roz didn't like taking orders from Lee, but she disliked watching dragons feed even more so she did as she was told. Locating the kitchen wasn't difficult; all she had to do was follow her nose. The outlying smells were savory: sesame oil, jasmine, garlic. Then came the earthy tang of vegetables plucked from a street vendor's stall. Finally, as she pushed aside a beaded curtain, the reek of rancid meat mixed with grease hit her. She gagged once and then again as the room came into focus. There was grunge everywhere: on the walls, the floor, the beat-up Formica counters. She did an about-face, meaning to wait out Brigit's feeding frenzy out in the shop, but before she could clear out, Lee showed up.

"Are you hungry?" she asked, as if she had not just caught Roz in mid-flight.

"No!" Roz said, almost but not quite suppressing a shudder at the mere thought of eating anything that came from this bio-hazard.

"You should eat," Lee went on, pulling unidentified objects from a darkened refrigerator. "It may be a while before the dragons are ready to begin negotiations."

The statement struck Roz as odd, even suspicious. "What is it that we're supposed to be negotiating?"

"Our next course of action, of course," Lee replied, as she dumped her UFOs onto the counter. "Why did you think Naga invited you here?"

"Truthfully? I thought she was just being a pain in the ass."

Lee made a noise deep in her throat. It could have been amusement. It could have been congestion. "Naga is Naga," she said. "There is always a reason behind her actions. If you will not eat, will you drink? We have whiskey."

It was becoming obvious to Roz that she wasn't going to be allowed out of the kitchen without a fight. And she just didn't have a fight in her after the last couple of days. So, with a sigh, she surrendered to the situation and said, "OK, I'll have a whiskey. Straight up--in a clean glass."

Then, suddenly cognizant of her weariness, she looked around for a place to sit. The only seat to be had was an old wooden stool that was being used as storage space. She relocated a bag of bok choy with a thumb and forefinger, half-expecting a swarm of roaches to come pouring out of it. She shifted a bunch of long beans as well and then brushed the dirty seat off before she sat down. Only then did she realize that Lee was watching her.

"I did not expect you to be so—dainty," she said, as she handed her the whiskey.

"Not dainty, just hygienic," Roz said, feeling free to return fire since Lee started it. "I have a thing about vermin."

"There are no vermin here," Lee replied, as she pulled a blackened wok from a pile of scorched pans and set it on a gas range that looked like it had never been cleaned.

Roz was so dumbfounded by the claim that it took her a moment to recover her voice. "Are you kidding me? Look at this place! It's a cockroach's wet dream!"

"This place is warded," Lee said, chopping up an onion with impressive speed. "Nothing can get in here if it hasn't been invited. I thought you would know that."

Now that Lee mentioned it, she did recall Brigit mentioning wards at some point in their past. She had assumed their purpose was to keep people out of a place, not critters. Besides, bugs weren't the only issue here. She rattled the ice in her glass like a diamondback getting ready to strike and then said, "So I guess the spell to keep grime away must have expired."

Lee snorted, an amused rather than offended sound, and set down her cleaver. "So self-righteous you are. So smug. Do you clean for your drakena?"

"Sometimes," Roz said, only to recall the cruise ship cabin that they had shared and the gigantic mess that they had created for housekeeping. Other memories followed: train sleepers, motel rooms, even her own bedroom, all of them dragon-trashed and all left for a maid. Slightly humbled, she added, "Not always, though."

"Yes," Lee purred, resuming her chopping. "I thought as much. My mother worked for people like you—rich white women who never cleaned up after themselves and yet considered themselves superior to the people who made their filth disappear." Before Roz could reject the association, Lee added, "I cook for Naga because I like to cook. Naga does not care if her food comes from a clean kitchen or a grimy one, so there is no issue."

"Maybe not for her," Roz said, "but what about you? What about—" She gestured at nothing in particular. "Germs?"

Lee tossed her chopped produce into the searing-hot wok. Over the ensuing hiss and sizzle, she said, "I grew up poorest of the poor. I am on excellent terms with germs. And dragons are not susceptible."

A bevy of incredible smells filled the room. To Roz's surprise and horror, her mouth began to water. Moments later, her stomach began to growl. Lee gave the wok one last expert toss and then cocked her head at Roz and said, "Will you eat?"

She had planned to pass. Her brain urged her to decline. Then a bowl heaped with sautéed vegetables and tofu appeared under her nose. The next thing she knew, she was shoveling stir-fry into her face with utter abandon. The chopsticks didn't slow her down even a little. Afterward, she was both embarrassed and dismayed.

"I don't know what got into me," she said, as she handed her empty bowl back to Lee. "I know I eat fast, but that had to be a land-speed record."

"The end of the age is coming," Lee said, pitching the dishes into an overfull sink. "All sorts of dragon appetites increase at such a time. Ours will increase as well."

"Great," Roz said. "The last thing I need is an appetite stimulant!"

Lee gave her a critical once-over. "You are tall and well-made. It may be that the extra weight will not show on you."

Roz made a rude noise and said, "I'd rather be small and compact like you."

Lee snorted over a cup of dragon tea and then let out a titter that was at extreme odds with her fierce outer persona. The fact that she was laughing both surprised and annoyed Roz, mainly because she had the distinct feeling that Lee was laughing at her. She gave the ice in her glass another rattle and said, "What's so funny?"

Lee paused for the briefest of moments as if she were unsure of her reply. Then, decision made, she locked eyes with Roz and said, "I haven't met many people who want to be like me."

The vulnerability embedded in that confession provoked a flash-bang moment in Roz. It lit up all her prejudices like tracer fire and then blew them straight to hell. "Yeah well," she said, "there aren't a lot of people clamoring to be like me, either." She rattled her ice a third time and added, "Can I get a refill?"

Wordlessly, Lee stood up and fetched the whiskey bottle. With one hand, she poured for Roz. With the other, she gestured at the dragon tattoos that adorned Roz's forearms. "It is easy to see the dragon in you," she said then. "The same cannot be said for your mother. How could she have had a Great One in her head for so long and not hear the Call?"

Roz shrugged. "Quetzalcoatl was old beyond reckoning. From what I understand, their primary connection was through the Dreaming. Mom thought it was just her imagination acting up. It wasn't until The Great One showed up on our doorstep that she got the full picture."

"Is Brigit a Dreamer?" Lee asked, oddly guarded in her curiosity.

"Nah," Roz replied, resisting the urge to add a heartfelt, 'Thank God!' "When she hits the hay, she goes down deep and stays there. My familiarity with the Dreaming is all second-hand."

"Naga does not ride the Dreaming often," Lee said in a distant voice. "When she does, I try not to be around. It never takes me anywhere I like to go."

"How old where you when you heard Naga's Call?" Roz asked, wondering if their stories were at all similar.

Lee studied Roz for a moment, pretty eyes narrowed as if she were searching for ulterior motives. Then, all at once, something opened or perhaps broke free within her and words started pouring out. "Naga did not Call me. I happened into her shop one day, looking for something to steal. I was twelve, a feral chimera. The people in Chinatown both feared and loathed me. I put a cloisonné pin in my pocket. An instant later, Naga grabbed me by the shoulder with a rock-heavy hand. I braced myself for the beating I thought would come next. Instead, she started sniffing me as if I were a bouquet of flowers. "I thought all of your blood were dead," she said, and I could feel her wonder flowing through me like warm water. Although I did not willingly share such things, I found myself saying, "I am the last."

"Wait!' Roz said, a friendly challenge. "What about your mom? You said she cleaned for rich white women." She deliberately left out the 'Like me'.

"She did—until she died of the damage that the Khmer Rouge inflicted on her before she fled Cambodia."

"Holy shit!" Roz said then, stunned by what she had just heard. "Your mom escaped the killing fields? What a crazy-harrowing experience that must have been! Were you with her? No, you couldn't have been, you don't look that old."

"Now I see your mother in you," Lee said. "She, too, has a fascination for stories. I did not talk to her because I do not understand her. But you—you are different. You have a dragon's heart, as do I. If you wish a glimpse into my past, I will give it to you."

Emotions crashed through Roz like a set of waves: after-the-fact embarrassment for being so off-handedly nosy: a sense of privilege for being trusted with someone's personal history; and then, more curiosity. "I'd like that," she said.

"My mother was the youngest of five. The three men became merchants like their father; the two women were given access to higher education. They all lived in Phnom Penh, which was known as 'The Pearl of Asia'—until the ascendant Khmer Rouge began shelling it. My mother and her family endured the bombardment for over a year, because the capitol was their home and they did not want to lose everything that they had built and owned. They kept telling themselves that things would eventually get better if they made do and kept their heads down.

The day the Khmer Rouge overtook Phnom Penh, they began evacuating the city, telling everyone to head for the countryside before American bombs started falling. When my mother's parents refused to leave, saying they were too feeble to travel, Khmer soldiers bashed their skulls in with their rifle-butts. The rest of the family needed no further prompting. They, along with two million others, fled the city carrying their valuables and bags of rice. The going was hard, for the road was crowded and the heat, intense. My mother's sister was pregnant and could not keep up. The family decided that she and her husband and their two children should take shelter at a small commune while the rest continued on to Battambang. My aunt was never seen again. Naga says she was buried alive."

Roz pressed a hand to her mouth, trying to keep her horror to herself. "Oh my God," she said. "I'm so sorry."

Lee shrugged. "It was before my time. And mercifully, my mother never knew. But even if she had, it would have only been one more loss to bear. Her youngest brother died of dysentery and exhaustion. Soldiers killed her middle brother in passing for not getting out of their way fast enough. By the time she and her last surviving brother reached Battambang, all of Cambodia was on the verge of starving. They decided to flee to Thailand. They were almost to the border when my uncle stepped on a landmine. The explosion killed him instantly and knocked my mother out. When she came to, she found herself on a cot with her belly stitched together. An old white man with kindly blue eyes was staring down at her. In heavily accented Khmer, he introduced himself as her surgeon.

"'You were lucky,' he told her. 'A Thai patrol was in the area when the mine went off. They brought you here before you bled out. I picked most of the shrapnel out of you before I closed you up, but I'm afraid some fragments are going to be with you for the rest of your life.'

"Out of gratitude, she spent the next five years assisting the surgeon in his refugee camp hospital. Then he fell sick with malaria and was told to go home. Before he left, he promised to advocate for my mother and bring her to America to live. She never saw him again. One year went by, then two. She continued her work as a hospital aide. The third year, a piece of shrapnel in her shifted and she lost a kidney. Year four dawned. The camp was overcrowded and infested with gangs. The leader of the Khmer Cobras tried to coerce my mother into stealing drugs from the infirmary for him. When she refused, he raped her. A week later, cleared for resettlement, she was taken from the camp and put on a boat for America.

"Nine months later, she gave birth to me alone in a one room tin shack on the outskirts in Stockton, California."

"Wow," Roz said, never more aware of—or grateful for— her privileged life. "Your mom was one tough woman."

"Indeed," Lee said. "In Cambodia, she had been an educated woman. Here, she cleaned houses for almost no money—with me strapped to her back until I learned to walk. When I was six, she hired me out to local farmers. I set onions, cut asparagus, and picked strawberries in the spring. Later in the year, I picked cherries, apricots, and tomatoes. Every night when I got home, she made me study. 'The only thing worse than being poor is being poor and ignorant,' she used to tell me. 'You must be smart, Narong, and strong if you want to survive in this world.'

"Narong?" Roz asked.

"Narong was my birth name, after my uncle who died in the minefield. Lee is the name I chose for myself when I met Naga."

"And when was that?"

Lee inhaled deeply and seemed to sink into the memory. "The year was 2000—the last Year of the Dragon. My mother had died in a San Francisco hospital the year before, killed at last by that long-ago landmine. By then, I knew that my birth sex was wrong and I was starting to let my femaleness show. That was not acceptable in Chinatown, and many people, children and adults alike, tried to beat me for daring to be myself. I expected Naga to do the same when she caught me stealing. Instead, she looked me in the eye and said, 'Fear not. I see you. I know you. I Choose you.'

"It was," she concluded, "the best day of my life."

CHAPTER 9

The road was curvy and dark, lit up only by the Jaguar's headlights. Twice now, Charles had had to brake for jaywalking critters: a fat-bottomed racoon first, militantly resolved to cross at its own dignified, old-mannish pace, and then a soft-eyed doe that bounded out of the gloom and toward the lake like a ballerina. Charles followed her with his eyes for a moment, thinking of a different time and a different deer. He could see why Aurora had liked this part of the world; it felt peaceful, idyllic. Under other circumstances, he probably would have liked it, too.

"Dude," Aldo said. "Why are we stopping? Mapquest says the place is still a quarter-mile down the road."

Charle squeezed the steering wheel with a certain someone's throat in mind. If that idiot called him 'dude' one more time.... He breathed in through his nose, calming himself. When this hunt was over and done, he could entertain every murderous thought that crossed his mind. Until then, he needed to stay focused. First things first.

"We'll walk from here," he said, parking the car on the side of the road. Then, because Aldo was still glued to his phone, he opened the glove box and said, "Stash your cell in there."

"What?" Aldo bleated. "Why?"

"Because I don't want anything giving us away," Charles said. "And your need to check your phone every two minutes tends to override your common sense."

"I'm checking for messages from Roz," Aldo said, in a tone that was both defensive and petulant. "You never know, she could get back to me. I sent her enough texts."

"Doesn't matter at this point," Charles said, and then handed over his own phone. "Here, put mine away, too."

If the gesture appeased Aldo, he didn't let on. Indeed, he started whining again as soon as he got out of the car. "Dude! It's fucking freezing out here!"

"Don't be a baby," Charles said, as he popped the trunk of the Jag. "It's not that cold."

"Is too! And I'm not dressed for an Arctic expedition. I think I'd better stay with the car while you go and—you know—do your thing. I'll be the getaway driver."

"Nuh-uh," Charles said. "I brought you here to identify Aurora Vanderbilt's daughter and watch my back, and that's exactly what you're going to do." He hefted his murder bag out of the trunk, eased the lid shut, and then added, "Move it. And keep your voice down. Sound carries over water."

They walked on the lake side of the road, Charles in front and Aldo somewhere to the rear. The lake glimmered by the light of a mostly full moon, but everything else seemed to be preternaturally still. In spite of his intention not to, he thought of Aurora again. For a moment, he could almost feel her presence beside him. Some mothers did that, tried to lure a predator away from their helpless offspring. He appreciated the effort, but it wasn't going to work. Tezcatlipoca was hungry for an offering, and his high priest was going to give him one.

"Holy shit! Look at the size of that cat!"

An instant later, Aldo appeared at Charles' elbow looking wide-eyed and overstimulated. "Did you see that?" he said, panting as if he had just run miles instead of yards. "It looked like a black panther!"

Charles supposed that there could be cougars in the area; the surrounding countryside was wild enough. And if the big cat was dirty or wet, it might even look black in the dark. But more likely, the idiot had seen a bobcat or the like and was being theatrical again.

"Which way did it go?" he asked, subtle mockery.

"That way," Aldo replied, pointing toward the stretch of woodland to his left. "It prowled across the road, looking right at me the whole way, and then disappeared into the trees. It was one scary-looking beast, dude!Look, the hair on the back of my neck is standing straight up."

"Yeah well," Charles said, thoroughly uninterested in the moron's scruff. "Whatever you saw is gone now, so settle down. We're coming to the end of the road." In more than one way, he hoped.

The cottage was set well back in the woods, but even from the top of the long, graveled driveway, Charles could tell that it was occupied. The outlines of a lamp glowed in the curtained front window; the stone chimney-top was oozing fragrant curls of smoke. The front door faced the road, and the soft yellow porch light was ablaze.

"Let's go around to the back and see what's there," Charles whispered. "I'd rather not go in the front way if we don't have to."

"Whatever, dude."

They prowled through a patch of forest that abruptly gave way to the lake's rocky shore, then followed the shoreline until it brought them to an upward sloping backyard that boasted a multi-level deck. The redwood decking looked vaguely skeletal in the moonlight. The terraces were bare, winterized perhaps or perhaps decommissioned. The barrenness both surprised and saddened Charles, for he had come to expect everything about Aurora to be filled with life. Then irony cleared its throat and his sadness took a bitter turn. He thumped Aldo in the chest to get his attention and then pointed to the unlit door at the top of the zig-zag stairway.

"We'll go in that way," he whispered. "I'll go first and access the situation. If the dragon is on the premises—"

"She's the enormous redheaded bitch," Aldo chimed in, perking up now that the time for action was drawing near. "The smaller one is Roz—and she's all mine. Remember? You promised."

"Yes, yes," Charles said, irked by the interruption. "But you can't kill her until we have the drakena under wraps." And by that, he meant drugged to the gills, courtesy of the carfentanil darts that he had bought on the black market. One was potent enough to drop a bull elephant in its tracks. It would probably take two to drop the drakena—or possibly three if she was as big as Aldo claimed—but down she would go. After that, the moron could do as he pleased with his former girlfriend. "Remember, they're linked psychically. If you hurt her before we have a bead on the dragon, the dragon's going to sense it and either fly off or come looking for blood. Either way, we're going to be fucked. You savvy?"

"Yeah, yeah," Aldo said, in a tone that sounded like details, details. "So long as I get to cap Roz at some point, I'm good."

Aldo's use of movie gangster jargon fanned Charles' irritation, but rather than abuse the idiot for it, he pulled the pieces of his high-powered rifle out of his duffel and put them together. "Wow!" Aldo gushed, when the rifle was fully assembled. "Nice piece! What about me? What do I get?" When Charles stared at him, his expression a big, fat 'nada', Aldo bleated, "Come on, I'm gonna need a gun to take Roz out. And what if that panther comes back?"

Charles glanced the strip of wooded shoreline to their rear. It didn't seem like a big cat's preferred hunting grounds. Hell, he wasn't even convinced that Aldo had actually seen a puma. But, if there was one thing that Charles had learned from his brief association with this idiot, it was that he'd bolt at the first odd sound if he felt the least bit threatened. And, galling as it was, Charles needed the idiot around for a little while longer. So, despite a boatload of reservations, he reached into the duffel again and pulled out a Glock.

"You know how to use one of these, right?" he asked. "Just point and click. Try not to shoot yourself—or me," he added, as Aldo wrapped his hand around the grip.

"Sure thing," Aldo said, seemingly mesmerized by the gun. "Whatever you say."

I wish, Charles thought, and then shifted the rifle to patrol ready position. "OK, I'm going in. Stay put until I give you the all-clear."

Stair by stair, he made his way up the deck. Although it was a cool night, a chorus of late-season peepers serenaded him along the way. As he set foot on the mid-level terrace, a glimmer of soft, deflected light caught his eye. Could it be? Yes! The door was open a crack! But—was that a good thing? Or bad? He resisted the urge to hurry, and now, after each step, he stopped to listen for dragon sounds. At the door, he paused for a nerve-steadying moment and then widened the crack with the tip of his rifle. The door let out a tiny, haunted house creak. An instant later, the frogs quit singing. He sucked in an oh-shit breath and tapped his trigger guard, waiting for the terrible clamor that came with a charging dragon.

But—nothing.

Heart-pounding moments later, the frogs resumed their serenade.

Shit! It was nights like this that made a career in dentistry look mighty good.

He continued widening the crack, inch by inch, until finally he was able to slip through it. The space in which he found himself was indirectly lit and smelled of caramelized onions, beef, and thyme: French onion soup. That had been one of Aurora's favorites. It was no surprise that the daughter had similar tastes. He glanced at the sink in passing: a pan, a cutting board, a single soup bowl. Nothing dragon-sized. He could not decide if he was disappointed or relieved.

A flicker of orange light caught his eye: a fire dancing in the living room hearth. A plaid couch spanned the length of the fireplace; someone was wedged into its near corner. Although that someone was wearing a knit cap, Charles could tell that he was stalking a woman. The elusive daughter. At last.

Unfortunately, her dragon did not appear to be with her.

He took a step forward. The floorboard groaned. The woman swiveled toward the sound, her movements brisk with alarm. An instant after she laid eyes on him, she did a double-take and said, "Charles?"

Aurora was ensconced on the couch in front of a crackling fire with a notebook on her knees. She'd been like that for an hour now, but the only thing that she had managed to write in that span of time was, 'Chapter One'. Her muse was dead. Nothing wanted to come out of her head, not even the sad, disconnected feelings in which she was wallowing. She wanted an outlet, but lacked focus. She wanted to purge, but lacked motivation. She scolded herself: a smart woman would give up this pathetic charade and go to bed. But she was stubborn, not smart. And there was a chance---'No promises!'---that Roz would be home tonight. With any luck, she'd arrive before Max and Mara returned from their Sacramento excursion. That way, Aurora could have a little alone time with her intrepid daughter. Did such a selfish hope made her a bad person?

CHAPTER 10

The chorus of peepers that lived down by the lake went suddenly quiet, signaling a new presence in the area. Aurora's first thought was: Roz! But even as her heart did a happy dance, logic tried to intervene: wouldn't she go to the front door?

Hope fired back: not if Brigit was in dragon form!

Her sudden agitation attracted an alien thought. *"Why so excited?"*

The intrusion made Aurora wince. Unlike Quetzalcoatl, who had had a subtle touch, Sadie was a bull in a cerebral china shop. She barged into Aurora's headspace, subtle as a tank, and broadcasted her wants and needs like a hungry child. She also eavesdropped—a lot. It got to be a bit much sometimes. Tonight, though, Aurora made an effort to be patient.

"The peepers stopped singing," she replied. *"I thought maybe Roz was home."*

"This one stopped the peepers," Sadie said.

"Oh," Aurora said, trying not to transmit her disappointment. *"What are you doing out there?"*

"Hunting." The thought was basted with drool and spiced with blood-salts.

"Go forth then," Aurora said, *"and catch yourself something tasty. The back door is open for you when you're done for the evening."*

Their connection shifted, a sensation like immersion. Aurora caught a whiff of the night: water, woodsmoke, vegetal decay. She felt tall grasses brush against her body and mud yield beneath her feet. And then—nothing. With a bit of effort, she could have sustained the link, but who wanted to be on the party line while a dragon was shopping for supper? She settled back into the corner of the couch and pulled out her cell phone, meaning to query Mara about her ETA. To her surprise, Mara had already left a text for her.

'Hi, Aurora! It took us longer than expected to find Max's computer doohickey, so we decided to spend the night here in Sac! See you tomorrow!'

Aurora responded with a smiley-face emoji.

The peepers waxed silent again—mourning a fellow lakeside denizen, Aurora supposed. Although she felt bad for whatever creature it was that had just lost its life, she knew a moment of pride, too, that maternalistic satisfaction that came with knowing baby could feed itself. *"Bon appetit, little one!"* she said, and then tensed as a loose floorboard in the kitchen creaked. At the same time, Sadie said, *"You did not tell this one you were expecting other humans!"*

Aurora's insides went cold. She knew with a certainty born of instinct that she had been found. All she could do now was limit the casualties. *"You stay away from here unless I Call,"* she said. *"If you see Roz, tell her to stay away, too."*

Then she flipped onto her knees and peered into the kitchen over the top of the couch. A figure phased into view, shadowy at first and then, as he moved into the fire's light, impossibly familiar.

"Charles?"

He looked as astonished as she felt.

"How—how did you find me?"

He continued to gape at her. She pulled off the cap that she had been wearing to keep her head warm and fumbled her way to her feet. Only then did she realize he was holding a rifle—and that it was pointed at her.

"What are you doing with that?"

The kitchen door swung open. An instant later, another man that she had never expected to see again stepped into view. Thoroughly confused now, she blurted the first thing that came to mind. "What are you doing here?"

"Good question," Charles growled, and then shifted to inflict a murderous side-eye upon Aldo fucking Whimsey. "I told you to wait outside until I waved you in."

Aldo shrugged. "I was cold. And I think that big cat came back. I didn't want to have to shoot it and maybe call attention to us."

Aurora glanced from Charles to Aldo and back again, trying in vain to make some kind of sense of a totally incomprehensible situation. "Would somebody please tell me what the hell is going on here?"

"We're looking for Roz," Aldo said, smirking at her over Charles's shoulder. "Where is she?"

"I don't know," she said, which is what she would have said regardless because there was no way she was going to let him drag her into this shitshow. She looked to Charles again, willing him to break his dogged silence and deliver the punchline that would turn this bizarreness into a very funny joke. "Are you going to say something or what?"

"I thought you were dead," he said woodenly. "You were supposed to be dead. I—never thought I'd see you again."

"That doesn't explain why you're here. Or why you're looking for my daughter with a gun in your hands and this chowderhead in tow."

Aldo's smirk shriveled into a snarl. He lifted up his shirt front and pulled a pistol from his waistband. "Can I shoot her?" he asked Charles. "Both she and Roz gotta go, right?"

Shock hit Aurora like a monstrous bitch-slap, leaving her red-faced and reeling. "Is this true?" she asked Charles, injecting all the heartache and gall that she was feeling into her voice.

"You're here to kill my daughter? I thought—" Part of her wanted to say the words, to validate the molten emotions that were already hardening into slag. The rest of her refused to take that much bitterness into her mouth. "I thought I knew you."

"I'm sorry, Aurora," he said. "This isn't—personal."

Aldo crowed. "Oh my God! I forgot you two were seeing each other. Dude, you are one cold motherfucker!"

"Zip it," Charles growled, but once Aldo started monologuing, there was no shutting him up.

"No, really! You had me torch your girlfriend's house! That's fucking frigid!"

Even with the assist, it took Aurora a moment to put two and two together. Even then, she didn't want to believe the math. He couldn't have. He wouldn't have. Finally, she had to ask. "Is that true?"

"Yes, ma'am!" Aldo said, oblivious to Charles' nuclear-grade scowl. "He gave the order, sure as shit. You can't blame him for the barn, though. The overgrown Esmerelda that you were hiding there lit that up just before a badass black dragon tore her open from chin to chest. I was there. I saw the whole thing! Your fat old dragon never stood a chance!"

Aurora had despised Aldo from the moment Roz had first introduced him, so it wouldn't have taken much to bump her up to hatred. Gloating over Quetzalcoatl's slaughter was pure overkill. For the first time in her life, she wanted not just to hurt another human being, but to inflict soul-searing pain: castration, evisceration, shattered bones. She took a step toward him, fists clenched. Charles urged her back with a thrust of his rifle.

"Aurora—"

The back door banged open, clipping Aldo in the shoulder. As he stumbled forward, Sadie-dragon burst into the cottage, chomped down on his calf, and jerked him off his feet. He hit the floor with a garbled scream. An instant later, she dragged him, thump-thump, over the threshold and into the night. Just before he disappeared, he stretched an imploring hand out to Charles and croaked, "Dude!" Charles strode over to the doorway, but all he did was stare out into the darkness and shake his head as if in amazement.

Aurora caught glimpses of Aldo's distress through Sadie: breathlessness and rising panic; the pain of punctured skin and torn muscle; hot blood spiked with adrenaline. Some inner voice way back in the cheap seats of her head whispered that she should be appalled by what she was sensing, yet she could not stop herself from savoring every psychic molecule. She wanted him to suffer. She wanted him to choke on his fear and—

A gunshot rang out. The sound skipped across the lake like a rock. Aurora felt a hot bolt of pain, a moment's surprise and then—flight. No further gunfire ensued. She released the breath that she didn't realize she had been clenching and then scowled as Charles called her back to the here-and-now.

"Did he get her?" he asked, looking irked by the prospect. When she declined to answer, he made a sour face and said, "Probably not. I don't think you'd be quite so composed if he had.

"Did she get him?"

"What's it to you?" she fired back. "You didn't even try to help him."

"Why would I?" he said, giving the great outdoors one long last look before shifting to give her his whole attention. "He outlived his usefulness. Your little dragon did me a favor by grabbing him."

Aurora choked back a laugh that was both incredulous and bitter. "You really are cold," she said. "And the truly frightening thing is, you hid it so well."

He waggled a finger at her in mock-reproach. "Now, now," he said. "I'm not the only one who's been less than forthcoming."

You managed to hide your affiliation with a Great One from me. And now it would appear that you've bonded with a second drakena. That's kind of unusual, isn't it?"

"Really?" she grated. "You killed my dragon, set fire to my home, conspired to murder my daughter—and now you want to chit-chat?" He broke her heart into a dozen more pieces with a shrug. "If you're going to kill me," she said, "just do it already. Lord knows, you wouldn't be the first to—" The tail-end of 'try' stuck in her throat, making it suddenly hard to breathe. "My God!" she grated. "That was you, wasn't it!"

To his credit, he didn't try to lie. "I had to," he said. "You knew—you know too much."

Every time she thought things were as mind-blowing as they could possibly get, they doubled down on her! "How absolutely galling, Charles," she said, in a stropped tone. "I wish I had never met you."

In response to that high-schoolish counterpunch, his expression softened. "Yes, I suppose you do," he said. "I can't say I blame you."

She averted her eyes, partly because the tender admission provoked unwanted feelings and partly because a thick tendril of green-gray fog was nosing its way through the battered door and she didn't want to give its presence away. Charles stared her for a distressingly long moment as if he were trying to penetrate her innermost defenses. When he finally spoke again, there was a hint of tension to his tone.

"This doesn't have to be the end, you know."

"What?"

The tendril reared up behind him, a definite threat display. A moment later, it sprouted a pair of lavender eyes. Now Aurora didn't know where to look. Charles didn't seem to notice. He was focused on his pitch, almost rapt.

"I mean it," he said. "Help me return the little drakena to her home. She'll be much easier to transport if you're around to keep her calm. Tezcatlipoca will reward you with your life for your assistance. Once he's pardoned you, we could put all of this unpleasantness behind us and start over again somewhere new."

But as much as she wanted to make that point uncomfortably clear, she kept it to herself. She saw an opportunity here, one that called for honey rather than toxic waste.

"You're asking me to trust you," she said. "With my life. After everything that's been done."

"I know," he said, solemn as a bridegroom.

"You want trust, you have to give trust," she went on, looking him straight in the eye. "I'm not going anywhere until you get rid of the rifle."

He hesitated, but only for a moment. The gun clattered to the floor. He kicked it toward the darkened dining room for good measure. There," he said. "What else?"

She looked up at Brigit and said, "OK. Do it."

CHAPTER 11

"Unbelievable," Roz said, as she walked a slow circle around her F-150. "You killed my truck again!"

"How the feck can ye be surprised?"" Brigit asked, projecting sardonic amusement. "Did ye think something had changed between this time an' tha last? An' let's not forget—yer tha one who wanted ta drive. A wanted ta go my way. All this movement without exertion is making me a wee bit flabby."

Roz gave the nearest tire a peevish kick. "In case you didn't notice, there's nothing resembling cover between San Francisco and Sac," she said. "Without cover, long-distance bounding in broad daylight would seem to be an ill-advised proposition. Wouldn't you agree?" When Brigit deflected the question with a shrug, Roz switched to kicking roadside rocks and tried to dial back on the snark. "Happily, the terrain gets wilder from here on, so as soon as the sun goes down, you'll be able to do your thing after all."

"A dunna want ta wait till sundown," the drakena said. "A've been out of tha water fer too long. If A dunna have myself a good soak pretty quick, my wits are going ta dry up and blow away. A'm already feeling a bit fuzzy."

"I know," Roz said, truly repenting her pique now, "and I'm sorry. I really want to see my mom, too. But Naga—"

"Naga," Brigit interjected sharply, "holds no sway over my comings an' goings."

"Of course not," Roz hastened to say. "But she believes that there are drakes and drake agents still active in this area and I have no reason to doubt her. We can't afford to be careless."

"Feck," Brigit echoed, spitting the word out like a piece of gristle that had been caught between two molars. "A'm tired of skulking. A'm tired of having ta look behind me after each and every step. A want this feckin' business ta be done already so A can go back ta my loch and mess with tha tourists."

I wouldn't mind getting some semblance of my life back, either," Roz said. "Let's start with me seeing my mom and you getting a soak." Brigit a petulant snort. Roz clapped her on the back, ignoring the spangles of pain that then skittered up her arm. "If the last twenty miles of billboards are to be believed, there's a barbecue shack a just few miles up the road. I say we track it down and make the best of a crummy situation."

Brigit snorted again, but this time the sour note held a grudging hint of appeasement. "Fine," she said. "But yer buying."

"Don't I always?" Roz replied.

Roz had to admit: traveling by leaps and bounds beat driving by a mile, especially on a moonlit night. As soon as the drakena cleared Sacramento, majestic Mount Shasta spanned into view. Standing over fourteen thousand feet high, the dormant, snow-capped volcano dominated the skyline even from a distance. Even Brigit, usually blasé about landscapes that didn't involve water, was impressed.

"*It draws tha eye,*" she said, "*but each time ye see it is like tha first.*" A little while later, she added, "*It's both magnificent and intriguing. A'd not be surprised if a dragon lived there.*"

"Now that you mention it," Roz said, "I wouldn't be super-surprised, either. The native American tribes who lived in Shasta's shadow considered the mountain sacred. And there are those today who swear it's a magical place. That sounds like dragon country to me."

The mountain grew closer, then closer still. The terrain went from farmland to wooded lots to dense swaths of forest tracked with streams and rivers. Brigit began to twitch at the sight of water and kept saying, *"Is this it? Is this it?"* Roz kept responding, "Not yet! Not yet!" until finally, an expanse of moonlit water appeared beyond the treetops. "There!" Roz exclaimed. "One more bounce ought to put us right on Lake Siskyou's southern shore. Look for an elbow-shaped point to the east. That's where the cottage will be."

If the directions registered with Brigit, she did not acknowledge them. Her thoughts were waterlogged, a saturated blend of want and need. Nevertheless, she went up again an instant after coming down, and when the lake came back into view, she shifted slightly eastward. The forest thinned out and then turned into waterfront fringe. The fringe then gave way to beach. "There!" Roz said. "That's the point!"

The drakena soared over the beach and then cannon-balled into the lake, taking Roz with her. Roz surfaced, sputtering. She could feel Brigit swimming circles beneath her. The thoughts she was broadcasting were both ecstatic and relieved.

"Tha water's tha the perfect temperature! And look at all tha toothsome-looking fish!"

"I'm happy you're happy," Roz said, raking dripping hair away from her eyes. "But you could've set me down on the beach before you dove in, you know. I didn't particularly want to drop in on Mom soaking wet."

"Aurora willna mind," Brigit said. *"Now scoot. A'll catch up with ye in a day or two."*

The plan agreed with Roz. After the scare she'd had—*your mother's dead*—she would take all the alone time she could get with her mom. But even as she took her first stroke toward land, a firecracker-like bang rang out and then rippled across the lake. A moment later, a small, winged silhouette cleared the darkened scrub and flapped frantically away.

"Was that—Sadie?" Roz asked

"Ai," Brigit said, shifting from happy to grim. *"Somebody shot her. She's more scared than hurt, though."*

As soon as Roz heard 'shot her', she started swimming like a would-be Olympian. She didn't know why Sadie was here. She didn't know what, if anything, the drakena had to do with her mother. But if there was a dragon-slayer in the area, then Aurora could be danger, too!

"A'm comin', too," Brigit said, surfacing beneath Roz so Roz could ride piggyback rather than swim. *"A'll not lose ye to a bullet."*

Moments later, they were back on land and running along the shoreline in the midst of a fast-moving fogbank. *"This way!"* Roz said, sharing the back way to the cottage, a path that she had known since childhood. She wanted to add, 'Hurry!', but the drakena was already moving as fast as she could through the trees. *"There!"* she said, as they broke into a clearing. *"That's our place!"*

"I smell human blood," Brigit said, and paused to snuffle the ground. *"The trail leads away from the cottage."*

Please God, Roz prayed, let that be good news.

Then she saw the darkened outlines of a man standing in the cottage's back doorway. He appeared to be holding some kind of gun.

Shit!

She slid down from Brigit's back and took a step toward the deck only to be checked by the drakena. *"A'm going first,"* she said, a thought infused with absolute authority. *"A'll let ye know when it's safe ta join me."*

Roz wanted to argue. She wanted to object. But the sensible part of her had to admit that a thick-skinned dragon might actually be better suited to the circumstances than a soft, unarmed, emotionally jacked-up daughter. *"All right,"* she said, *"you go ahead. I'll watch your back. But keep your mind open so I can get a feel for what's going on, OK?"* When Brigit refused to agree, Roz gave her a slap on the flank, a reproach that hurt Roz like hell and had no noticeable impact on Brigit. *"I mean it, dragon, don't you dare shut me out! And stay off the third step—it squeaks."*

Brigit made no reply; she was already on the prowl disguised as fog with a solid center. The third stair made no mention of her passing. She stole closer to the man with the gun, then closer still. Then she extended her neck and looked over his shoulder, maintaining radio-silence for what seemed like an eternity. Roz wrung her hands into fists. She shifted her weight from one foot to the other and back again. When she could not stand the suspense any longer, she dared a thought.

"Is Mom in there? Is she OK?"

"She is here," Brigit replied, projecting calm. *"She is talking to this man. She doe nae appear tae be happy."*

"Is the gun pointed at her?"

"Ai, it would appear so." A heartbeat later, she added, *"Ah, she's seen me. Tha's a good thing, A think. She seems tae have all her wits about her."*

No surprise there, Roz thought. Her mother was rock-steady. Unlike her daughter, who was a hair away from losing her shit! It wasn't enough to be told what was going on. She needed to see for herself! She tiptoed up the first step and then the second, but all she could see was fog and the back end of a dragon.

"What's happening now?"

"Tha man is trying tae talk her into betraying Sadie. A believe A will kill him now."

"No!" Roz said. *"He might shoot Mom!"* A moment later, a huge pulse of surprise and curiosity rolled through her psyche. *"What was that?"*

"Aurora just persuaded tha man ta drop his gun! Now she's telling me to 'do it.' Do what, do ye suppose?"

"Bite him! Nonlethal, but just barely!" she added, as she felt the drakena snake in for the strike.

"Shite! He tastes good! And—" She growled, a psychic vocalization that did not bode well for the man. *"He stinks of drake!"*

Roz couldn't stand it any longer. She had to be in on the action! She bounded up the rest of the steps, patted Brigit's flank in passing to let her know she was there, and then ducked into the cottage. Aurora was standing next to the living room couch, looking pale and flushed. The man was dangling slightly off the ground with his right shoulder clamped in Brigit's sea-monster jaws. Despite his precarious situation, and despite the pain that the effort was obviously causing him, he was trying to retrieve his cast-off rifle with an extended toe. Crazy!

"I'd hold still if I were you," she said, as she slogged past him. "You strain too much and you'll tear a whole bunch of subclavian veins right out of your body. You wouldn't want to bleed out all over my mom's floor, would you?"

He was sweating now, a reaction to Brigit's venom, and his temple was telegraphing his pulse. Nevertheless, he only had eyes for Aurora. "I can't believe—you played me—like that," he panted, finding it hard to breath around a dragon's bite. "We—would have been—so good—together."

"I don't think so," Aurora said, and then folded Roz into a soggy embrace. "Oh my God," she whispered. "I'm so glad you're here."

"Me, too, Mom," Roz said, and then held her at arm's length for inspection. "You OK?" When Aurora responded with a nod, Roz off-gassed her worries with a sigh and then tousled her mother's already fly-away hair. "Geez," she said, "I leave you alone for a few days and you wind up in a hostage situation! Who is this guy anyway?"

"Charles," Aurora said, in a wincing tone that turned bitter at the end.

"Your Charles?" Roz asked, a bug-eyed query. "What's he doing here? And what's with the rifle?"

"He's the drake agent who compromised me," Aurora said. "He came here expecting to kill you."

Charles let out a strangled groan: the sound of Brigit tightening her bite in response to the revelation. Roz flashed the drakena a quick thought—*"Easy now!"*—and then jumped back into her conversation with Aurora. "How did he know that I'd be here? Max and Mara were the only ones who—" Knew, she meant to say, but a terrible afterthought derailed her. "Oh my God, are they OK? Did he—?"

"They're fine," Aurora said, firmly stubbing out that spark of panic. "It was Aldo. Aldo led him here. Don't worry," she added, as Roz checked the dark corners of the cottage for signs of her ex. "He's gone. Sadie dragged him off."

Her dread receded, leaving her aggrieved rather than relieved. She stared at her would-be murderer for a long moment, taking in details that her brain refused to process. All she could see was a stranger who had come to kill her. "What are we supposed to do now?" she asked at last. "Call the cops?"

"I don't think so," Aurora said coldly. "He's a drake agent. Given the proper motivation, I imagine he could tell us a useful thing or two."

"I agree with yer mum," Brigit said.

At the same time, Charles grated, "Not—likely."

"Don't be so sure," Roz said. "Brigit can be very persuasive."

He dismissed her with a glance and returned his attention to Aurora. His scowl was both fierce and tender. "If—the order

to—kill you—couldn't make me—betray—Tezcatlipoca—
what makes you think—a lesser pain—would?"

Aurora didn't know what to say to that. He didn't seem to mind.
"Sorry about the floor," he said, and then lunged toward Roz.

Flesh ripped. Blood spurted. Aurora croaked, "No!" but
it was already too late. He fell to the ground even as Brigit
released him. Despite the agony he must've felt in the last
moments of his life, his expression seemed curiously peaceful,
almost relieved.

"Jesus, Bridge," Roz said, as she gaped at the body. "What
part of nonlethal didn't you get?"

"This was nae my doing," Brigit replied, broadcasting surprise.
*"He triggered my bite reflex with tha sudden move. He was a drake
agent; he had tae have known that would happen."*

"Suicide by dragon?" Roz asked, and then glanced at Aurora.
"Does that sound like him, Mom?"

"I—don't know," Aurora said, as tears beaded in the corners
of her eyes. "He wasn't anything like the man I thought I knew."
She covered her mouth with a hand and sobbed before adding,
"He did apologize about the floor, though."

The sight of Aurora choking up both distressed and angered
Roz. "C'mon, Mom," she said. "This guy doesn't deserve your
tears. He was here to kill us!"

"I know, I know," Aurora said, dabbing at her eyes with the
back of her hand. "I'm just a little stressed at the moment.
And—" She swallowed hard. "I wanted to hurt him so bad. I
really did. But I didn't want him dead. Not really."

Roz studied the body for a moment, trying to put herself in
her mother's shoes. If that had been Aldo sprawled there on the
floor, would she be wringing her hands and fighting back tears?
Nope. Not even close. If anything, she'd be a little giddy. *See
what you get for fucking with me?*

Brigit mocked her for the thought. *"Yeah, right. A offered ta make tha halfwit disappear on several occasions, but ye wouldna have it. Yer just as tender-hearted as yer mum."*

"Nuh-uh," Roz said, for lack of a pithier comeback. Then, uninterested in pursuing the digression further, she returned to the matter at hand. "Whether you wished it so or not, Mom, the guy's dead. The question now is, what do we do with the body?"

"A'll carry him into tha lake," Brigit said. *"A'll take him someplace deep and dark and secure him there. Fish will nibble him down tae tha bone."*

Roz relayed the offer to Aurora, all but the part about the nibbling fishes. Aurora signaled her approval with a solemn nod and said, "We'll clean up while you're gone."

"No need ta rush tha scrubbing on my account," Brigit told Roz. *"After A stash tha meat, Am going ta find a patch of lake bottom and have a snooze. Look fer me in a day or two."*

"Before you check out," Roz said, *"you'd better get in touch with Naga. Tell her to get out here as soon as she can."*

Brigit opposed the suggestion with a psychic scowl. *"Why? We dunna need her help. We took care of the problem."*

"True," Roz conceded. *"But taking care of our problems one by one isn't getting us any anywhere. I think it's time we took a different approach. I think it's time to go for the throat."*

"Ye say that like something's changed."

"Something has," Roz replied, breaking into a sly grin. Before Brigit could ask, she added, *"We know where Sadie is now. That little dragon is the game-changer."*

Roz felt doubts bubble up in the drakena only to fizzle into a swarm of weariness. *"A'll Call her if that's what ye want,"* she said. *"But mark my words: she'll find a way ta complicate any plan ye might have. Ye know she likes her drama."*

"I know," Roz replied, starting to feel fatigued, too. *"But let's*

worry about that when she gets here. Go. Enjoy your rest. And—thanks for saving mom's life."

Brigit snorted. "*You and yer thanks. A'd rather have a bottle of Scotch.*"

With that, she took Charles' ruined shoulder in her jaws and began to drag the body out the equally ruined doorway. As she did so, Roz heard a strangled gasp to her rear. She turned to find her mother watching the grisly business. She looked fragile again, pale and near to tears, but she did not look away until her ex-lover's heels thumped over the threshold and disappeared into the night.

"Damn!" she said then, running a hand through her tousled hair. "Every time I think things can't get any worse, the universe rushes in to prove me wrong." She turned her shipwrecked gaze on Roz and asked, "When's it going to end?"

"I don't know, Mom," she said, folding Aurora into a bearhug. "Soon, I hope." She held her mother tight until she started to relax and then tried to lighten the mood. "On the bright side," she said, "Aldo is finally out of our hair." Aurora shook her head. "We don't know that yet. We need to look for his body."

Roz groaned. Just what she wanted to do after traveling forever and a day. As much as she wanted to blow the job off, though, she knew she couldn't. "OK," she said, only to be struck by an afterthought. She eased Aurora out of their embrace and looked her in the eyes. "You said Sadie dragged Aldo away. How do you know her? What was she doing here?"

Aurora shrugged like a kid who's been asked something simple. "Saidhe lives here," she said. "She's my dragon."

"At last!" Roz exclaimed. "Some good news!"

CHAPTER 12

"*Can I shoot* her?" The thought of putting a big, fat hole in High-And-Mighty Aurora Vanderbilt gave Aldo a chubby. "Both she and Roz gotta go, right?"

The bitch flinched and then fixed disbelieving eyes on Charles. "Is this true?" she asked. "You're here to kill my daughter? I thought—I thought I knew you."

To Aldo's surprise and great delight, Charles flinched, too. "I'm sorry, Aurora," he said. "This isn't—personal."

Aldo couldn't believe his ears. Had Charles really just apologized to Aurora? Why? As he pondered the anomaly, a memory popped loose—and holy shit, what a memory it was! "Oh my God!" he said, leaping at the chance to make Mr. Tough Guy squirm. "I forgot you two were seeing each other. Dude, you are one cold motherfucker!"

"Zip it," Charles growled, but Aldo was just getting started. "No, really! You had me torch your girlfriend's house! That's fucking frigid!"

Aurora blinked several times like someone trying to wake up from a bad dream. "Is that true?"

"Yes, ma'am!" Aldo said, relishing the scowl that ridged Charles' brow. Someone didn't like the taste of his own medicine! "He gave the order, sure as shit. You can't blame him for the barn, though. The overgrown Esmerelda that you had stashed there lit that place up just before a badass black dragon opened her up from chin to chest. I was there. I saw the whole thing! Your fat old dragon never stood a chance!"

The sorrow avalanched from Aurora's face, leaving a façade of pure hatred behind. She started toward him with fists clenched and wildfire in her eyes. Charles checked her advance with a thrust of his rifle.

The back door banged open, knocking him off-balance. The next thing he knew, he was face-down on the floor and something had him by the leg. Shit! It had to be the goddamn cat! He yowled once as pain flooded his brain and then again as the cat started dragging him out the door. He reached out to Charles for help, but that asshole just stood there and watched as the cat hauled him away. Down one step he went, then another and another, his chin landing hard each time. Then, on the fourth step, the cat let go of his legend began clawing at his back—trying to flip him over, it seemed. He remembered the Glock then; it was still locked in his hand. Immediately, frantically, blindly, he rolled over and fired. The cat slashed his torso, a glancing swipe, and then—nada. Aldo scrabbled to his knees, then jerked the gun this way and that. It took him several heart-pounding moments to realize that the cat was gone. He'd scared it off, leastwise for now. And he sure as hell wasn't going to wait around for it to come back!

He forced himself to his feet and staggered down the last deck step only to trip and fall into the brush that bordered the yard. Shit! His leg, back, and chest felt like they were on fire! And his heart was pounding so hard, he thought for sure it was going to burst out of his ribcage. As he laid there in the tall grass, panting like an overheated dog, a thick blanket of fog drifted in from the lake. It crept up the steps that he had just been dragged down and then disgorged a long, sinuous shadow with a large, horse-like head.

Shit! That was the monster that he'd seen that night in the cruise ship hot tub! And—it appeared to be stalking Charles! Closer and closer to the doorway it crept, perfectly stealthy despite its size. Aldo thought about firing a warning shot, but—fuck that! Charles hadn't lifted a goddamn finger when Aldo needed help.

The dragon reared up, blocking Charles from view. Aldo held his breath, waiting for the beast to deliver a little comeuppance only to hiss as a second figure came stealing out of the fog. Although he couldn't see her face, Aldo recognized Roz's mannish contours instantly. He aimed the Glock at the space between her shoulder-blades and tapped its trigger-guard as he recounted his grievances against her. She'd lied about the monster, then mocked and gaslighted him when he pressed her. If she had told him the truth, he would have never fallen in with Charles, or been threatened, abused, and practically enslaved. His calf, back, and chest wouldn't be in flaming shreds. As much as he wanted to bust a cap in her, though, he held up—because of the dragon. He knew he wouldn't be able to outrun its wrath in his condition. He also knew how terrible a dragon's wrath could be. So, as Roz scampered up the deck steps, Aldo rolled onto his belly and commando-crawled his way through the brush. When he finally reached the street, he climbed to his feet and power-limped all the way to Charles's car. By the time he got there, he was sweaty, wheezy, and ready to barf.

He broke into the Jag because he wanted his phone back. And it wasn't really breaking in because he knew where Charles kept the spare key. Then it occurred to him that he needed a ride home. And Charles did kind of owe him for all the work that he had done. Besides, if things were proceeding the way Aldo imagined they were back at the cottage, Charly Boy wasn't going to be needing this fine set of wheels anymore.

As he was adjusting the driver's seat, his cell phone rang. He plucked it out of the glove compartment and pressed it to his ear on auto-pilot. An instant after he said, "S'up?" He realized that the ringtone was different.

"Who is this? Where's Carlito?"

The voice was unfamiliar but strangely compelling. Aldo found himself saying, "Carlito is most likely dead at this juncture."

"Dead?" The speaker sounded annoyed rather than mortified. "How?"

"Dragon got him," Aldo quipped.

"How do you know this? Who are you?"

Whoops. A normal person wouldn't have taken him seriously. Therefore, this had to be one of Charles' dragon pals. His stomach clenched. The sweat on his brow took a sudden chill. He snuck a peek at the rear-view mirror, half-expecting to see a flame-wreathed Drogo Channing closing in on the Jag's back end. What a relief it was to see nothing but ordinary darkness!

"I'm Aldo—Aldo Whimsey," he said, trying to keep the nervousness from his voice. "I guess you could say I was Charles' apprentice. We were taking care of a loose end when we were ambushed. A mountain lion got me and a dragon got him."

A savage hiss ensued, confirming Aldo's suspicion. "Where is the dragon now?"

"Probably still at the cottage," Aldo said. "That's where her people live."

"You must go back there and keep watch," the caller said—commanding, not asking. "If she leaves, you must follow her."

"No fucking way!" Aldo blurted, thoroughly done with the whole dragon scene. "I'm on my way to the hospital. Get someone else to be your watchdog."

"No!" the caller snapped—a sound like dry bone breaking. "I am Tezcatlipoca, god of darkness and magic. As you served Carlito, so now shall you serve me. I will reward you richly for your efforts."

Just like that, Aldo became acutely aware of the Jag's high-end interior: ergonomically designed seats, a sound system to die for, the smell of fine leather. No doubt about it, this ride had cost Charles a pretty penny. Aldo was between vehicles at the moment. Between jobs, too. 'Richly rewarded' sounded like a first-class ticket to a fresh start in New York City.

Maybe he wasn't done with dragons after all.

"I'm listening," he said.

CHAPTER 13

"Drogo Channing is not available to take your call. Please leave a message at the tone."

Tezcatlipoca roared at the cell phone and then hurled it across the chamber. The device hit the stone wall with a metallic thud and shattered. Stupid man-magic! Stupid Drogo! How dare he not be available when Tezcatlipoca had need of him? Tezcatlipoca roared again, venting frustration. Nothing was going right! Carlito was dead. Rasputin was incommunicado. Now Drogo was ignoring his calls. Fuck!

Carlito's loss was hugely inconvenient, but inevitable. A man working so closely with dragons was not likely to live to old age. And in truth, he had expected Drogo to betray him at some point. But Grishka? Grishka Rasputin had been with him from the start—his right-hand man, as Carlito might have said. He needed the lesser drake here to help with the wyrms, who were maturing in very peculiar ways.

The thought of his stable of would-be breeders instigated another complaint. He should have eaten that wretched pharmacist bit by bit instead of killing him outright! What had he been thinking, substituting human estrogen for dragon estrogen? Some of the wyrms were displaying disturbing predilections. Others seemed to have some form of arrested development while others still had sexed male in spite of the hormone treatments. He knew what Grishka would have to say about the situation—some cleverly phrased form of 'I told you so'. But he'd also work his magic on the surviving wyrms and mold them to Tezcatlipoca's purpose just as he had roused them from their icy slumber.

He was close, so close to realizing his ambition! Why was everything falling apart now?

A lesser drake might have despaired. Tezcatlipoca, however, had no intention of giving up. Indeed, if that apprentice of Carlito's did as he was told, then the loss of a few wyrms or even the entire clutch, would be of no consequence. Tezcatlipoca would have a full-grown drakena with which to restock the next age! Aldo Whimsey could make him a god again!

If he could find a drake to help the human out.

With a surly snarl, Tezcatlipoca went hunting for the box of cell phones that Carlito had laid in store for him. Such a clever, capable man that one had been. Hopefully, he had trained his successor well.

CHAPTER 14

"Did you just ignore a call from the Great One?" Wo Long asked, expressionless save for a slight rise in one delicate eyebrow.

Drogo took one long last drag from his cigarette and then flicked the still-burning butt into the busy street. "Yes," he said, bathing the word in smoke. "Yes, I did. The Great One likes to micromanage. It becomes wearisome quicker than you might think. Fret not," he added, as the arch in the mandrake's eyebrow grew more pronounced. "I'll fill him in on our findings as soon as we return to the states."

Wo Long nodded. "He is wise to keep his options open. So much could go wrong with a resurrected clutch of biochemically altered wyrms."

"Too true," Drogo said, a smug little rumble. "Too true. We'll need an agent on the inside for this, someone who has access to the secret research labs. Do you know anyone?"

"Most assuredly," Wo Long said.

"It can't be a drake," Drogo said. "There's too much time and tedium involved. Also—"

Wo Long looked down his well-appointed nose and cracked an amused half-smile. "What was that you were saying about micromanagement?" When Drogo stiffened, projecting offense, the mandrake snorted and said, "Relax. I can get what you need. This is China. All it will take is money."

Drogo hmphed, grudgingly mollified, and then pulled another cigarette from his jacket. As he lit it up, an oversized limousine pulled up to the curb in front of them and Azi Zhahhak emerged from the cabin. "They are ready to receive us, Great One," he said. "Shall we go?"

Drogo cocked his head at Wo Long. "Are we done here?"

"We are," Wo Long replied, "except for a curiosity on my part." When Drogo nodded, granting him permission to air his itch, he said, "How did you find out about Wuhan in the first place?"

The question delighted Drogo. He sucked in a smoky breath, blew it back out through his nostrils, and then grinned. "The Center for Disease Control sent me," he said. "They want me to persuade the Chinese to let them help monitor and respond to potential pandemics."

Wo Long's long, thin mouth stretched into a long, thin smile. "The fox in the hen house." "

Precisely."

CHAPTER 15

There had been contact: a fleeting, long-distance, late-evening Call. *Come now!* Naga disliked having her rest disturbed. Naga disliked being ordered about even more. Nevertheless, Naga had roused Lee and they had flown through the night and well into the morning because the contact had bristled with urgency and Naga trusted the sender.

Lee spotted the first confirmation that all was not well. *"Look!"* she said, as Naga circled Aurora's hideaway in search of a place to land. *"The back entrance is boarded up."*

Naga rumbled, disgruntlement amplified by fatigue and hunger. *"I wonder how it is that trouble manages to find that woman everywhere she goes?"*

"I cannot imagine a drake patching up a doorway after he went through the trouble of demolishing it," Lee said, choosing to deflect rather than fan Naga's prejudices about Aurora. *"My guess is that she managed to drive her attacker off."*

"That is one possibility," Naga said, *"but certainly not the only one."* She landed on the cottage's roof, butterfly-quiet, then hopped down to the driveway and dropped one shoulder so Lee could dismount. *"I will go in first,"* she said—telling, not asking. *"You will wait here until I Call for you."*

Resentment coursed through Naga: Lee expressing her displeasure at being relegated to the rearguard. A second pulse followed a moment later—grudging acceptance mixed with spite. *"If you forget and leave me out here,"* she warned, as Naga started toward the front door, *"I will never cook for you again."*

Naga made no reply. She was in hunter mode now, ready to

engage. If there was a drake lurking within, she would bite his head off and eat the rest of him for breakfast. She prowled up to the door and gave it an exploratory nudge. To her surprise, it creaked open. The gust of air that greeted her smelled of woodsmoke, lemony cleanser, and red blood residues. Her mane stiffened. Fiery potential awoke in her belly. She barreled into the cottage with a roar, daring any and all to challenge her.

In response, an iridescent lump in front of the blazing fireplace stirred, lifting its head ever so slightly up from the nest of its forearms. An instant later, a presence barged into her awareness. *"Are you Naga? Why so loud?"*

The fire in Naga's belly fizzled, doused by surprise. That iridescent lump was a young drakena! Naga stared for a moment, stunned to thoughtlessness by the novelty of the situation. Youth marked the beginning of an age, not its end. Then inspiration struck: this was the wyrm that had escaped Tezcatlipoca's clutches! The realization triggered a flood of questions.

"How did you get here? Are you the reason for the Call? What is your name?"

"Saidhe is this one's Divine-given name," the drakena said politely enough, *"but most everyone shortens it to Sadie. This one followed Aurora here. We are bonded. This one knows nothing about a call."*

The mention of Aurora triggered another cascade of wonder and irritation in Naga. That woman! A week ago, Naga had contemplated killing her for the sin of surviving her dragon. A week ago, Naga had considered her to be without value, a risk, possibly a danger. Now here she was, dragon-less no more—and still possibly dangerous.

"Where is Aurora?" she asked.

"She went to a people-place to do people-things," Sadie said. In response to the flash of irritation that escaped Naga, she added, *"She did not expect you so soon."*

Under different circumstances, Naga might have admitted that the thermals had been her favor. Here and now, she bristled instead, supremely irked that Aurora had underestimated her. She was so irritated she forgot to keep it to herself. Lee responded with a flash of her own pique and then marched into the cottage only to skid to a stop when she saw Sadie.

"Who do we have here?" she asked, radiating surprise rather than alarm.

"*This is Sadie,*" Naga replied, reining in her sour mood. "*The runaway who got away. She is bonded with Aurora.*"

"How interesting," Lee said, and joined Naga in studying the drakena. Saidhe was small, dramatically so, even for one so young. Her coloring was flashy. There was a lively gleam in her eyes, but Naga suspected that her intellect was as stunted as her body. Why else would she bond with a leftover like Aurora?

Lee pointed at a gash that spanned the length of Sadie's left shoulder. "What's that?"

The youngling's scars did not interest Naga, but Lee wanted to know, so Naga asked. Sadie's response was as blasé as Naga's query. "*Aurora says it is the mark of a bullet that did not quite miss. This one does not know what that means.*"

See? Dim. Just as Naga had surmised. "*It means that someone tried to kill you.*" But why would a drake agent do that? Tezcatlipoca wanted her captured, not dead. The only explanation that made sense was that her injury had been an accident. Perhaps the agent, like Naga, hadn't known that the youngling was here. He had come hunting for Aurora only to stumble into a dragon's lair. When confronted by a drakena, even a runt like Sadie, all but the most stout-hearted of humans could reasonably be expected to abandon their mission and do whatever it took to preserve their lives.

"*Did you kill him?*" Naga asked, unable to tell from the diluted floorboard residues.

"Him who?" Sadie replied.

"The man who was here last night," Naga said, straining for patience despite her hunger and fatigue and natural inclination to the contrary.

"Which one?"

Aiya! This *ben dan* was even duller than Naga had imagined! *"How many were there in all?"*

"Two," Sadie replied offhandedly, growing bored with her grilling.

"Were both destroyed?"

"Who can say?"

That tiny show of disrespect shattered the last of Naga's restraint. With a deftness honed by centuries of experience, she shouldered past the boundaries that defined a polite exchange and lodged herself deep in Sadie's mind. *"Show me what happened."*

Unable to resist or evade, Sadie began pumping images mixed with sensation into Naga's head. Darkness and hunger pangs came first, along with hunter's tunnel-vision. Then: flickers of movement in Aurora's backyard—a pair of unfamiliar silhouettes creeping toward the door. One entered, inciting confusion-not-her-own. The other entered, provoking a white-hot hate that filled the mouth with a hunger for blood. Instinct erupted. The next thing she knew, she was dragging a man out of Aurora's place and into the darkness. He was bigger than her usual prey; heavier, too. His struggles to escape excited her. She flipped him over, eager for the kill. A terrible flash-bang greeted her. She squawked with surprise and pain, then bolted into the sky.

Satisfied, Naga released her mind-grip on Sadie's memory. The youngling shivered from head to tail, offloading stress, and then hissed at Naga. *"That was rude."*

Naga mocked her with a snort. *"The man who shot you was still alive when you fled,"* she said. *"What about the other? That has to be his blood I am smelling in the floorboards."*

"He was gone when this one returned this morning. Aurora did not say where he went."

The answer irked Naga, but before she could express her displeasure, a set of vibrations from without caught her attention. There was no guile to the sensations, no hint of stealth. That suggested friend rather than foe and certainly not drake. Nevertheless, she directed Lee into the relative safety of the kitchen and then struck her most intimidating pose. The front door swung open. A man and a woman stepped into the cottage, each of them carrying a duffel bag. The man dropped his burden an instant after he laid eyes on Naga, then clutched the woman's arm as if he were in sudden need of support.

"Please, Mara!" he whispered. "Tell me we know this one."

Mara kissed the man on the cheek and said, "Steady, Max. We're all friends here." Then she eased herself out of his grip and waved. "Hello, Naga! Nice to see you again! You're even more spectacular as a dragon than you are as a woman. And you, you little dickens," she added, peeking around Naga and toward the hearth, "are you going to come and say hi or what?"

Sadie let out a happy warble and charged. An instant later, Mara was on her backside with the drakena on top of her. She laughed as if there weren't an apex predator sitting on her chest and gave the tops of said predator's eye-ridges a delicious-looking scratch. "Good to see you, too, Sadie," she said. "You're such a pretty girl."

Naga was scandalized and immediately pulsed a thought to Lee. Lee was quick to pass the message on. "Naga says to stop treating Saidhe like a pet. She is a dragon not a puppy, and needs to learn to think like one."

"I'll treat her like a friend," Mara said, a declaration both sweet and emphatic. "Because that's what she is. Hopefully, that will make her a well-adjusted dragon."

Naga snorted, grimly amused. What were the odds of a stunted, out-of-time drakena with a hand-me-down human turning out well-adjusted?

"I don't mean to be rude," Max said, edging toward the kitchen, "but I hear we have a door to fix."

Naga ignored him, and why not? The door's condition was of no concern to her. Indeed, the only concern she had at the moment was her dreadfully empty belly. She pulsed a thought at Lee: *"Find me something to eat."* Then she settled down on the spot that Sadie had just vacated, intending to snooze until Lee made food appear. Lee looked to Mara, who was still on the floor with Sadie.

"Is there food in this place?" she asked.

"A little," Mara replied, and then giggled as Sadie nosed her for another scratch. "Aurora went out for more. She should be back any time now."

"Show me what you have on hand," Lee said. "Naga requires sustenance."

Mara knuckled Sadie's eye-ridges one last time and then shoved her onto the floor. The drakena let out a disappointed honk and then turned toward the fireplace only to realize that her spot had been commandeered. She honked again, an aggrieved reproach, then padded over to a corner and began huffing puffs of smoke into a mousehole. Naga kept track of the goings-on for a dozy moment, then allowed herself to sink deeper and deeper into slumber. As she descended, her dream-self peeled away from her body and hovered on the banks of an ethereal slipstream. Naga did not ride the Dreaming often, but today, she surrendered to its pull in the hope that it would sweep her back to a time and a place where Quetzalcoatl still lived. She wanted answers from the Great One. She craved—direction. But the Dreaming ignored her desires. First it flew her through a sky-colored kaleidoscope. Then it dumped her on the steps of a human homestead. The place was surrounded by old-growth redwoods, but it felt foreboding rather peaceful. There was a presence within. It was—waving at her. Beckoning her nearer? Or warning her away? As she debated her next move, she heard an otherworldly creak and then footsteps. A heartbeat later, a voice cried out, "There you are!" and the Dreaming rippled away without her.

"There you are, little one! Hunting for mice again, I see. How's that scratch today? Wow! that looks good! You're a quick healer!"

More voices intruded along with a host of shuffling and jostling sounds.

"Yay! You made it!"

"Oh my God, hello, it's so good to see you two again!"

"Here, Aurora, let me take those bags from you. How are you doing?"

Naga cracked one eyelid open, then the other. Aurora and Rosalyn were standing side by side in the kitchen. This was the first time that Naga had seen them together. Rosalyn was taller, with a firm, athletic build. Aurora sagged a little in places. Both had angular jaws and confident carriages. Both had the same smile. But where Roz was open-faced and easy to read, Aurora was closed off, resistant; a cypher. What purpose did her bonding with a second drakena serve? Why wouldn't the Divine make Her plan clear?

Although Lee was unpacking groceries in the kitchen, she sensed Naga's agitation and pulsed a reassurance. *"Food has arrived. There is chicken—and pig ribs! I will bring you some soon."*

The promise of sustenance failed to distract Naga. Her need for perspective was stronger than her appetite. *"Ask Aurora why she did not tell me that she had located Saidhe,"* she said. *"Ask her why she did not tell me that that they had bonded."*

Lee was so surprised by Naga's gustatorial indifference, she didn't even object to serving as Naga's mouthpiece.

Aurora listened respectfully and then shifted, making herself available for eye-contact with Naga. The left corner of her mouth was quirked; the opposite eyebrow was arched. "The last time we were in the same room together," she said, "you made it perfectly clear that ours was a don't-call-me-I'll-call-you kind of relationship. So, you don't get to cry foul about not being the first to know anything about me. But for the record, Sadie has only been here for a couple of days. And, it was she who found me, not vice versa. She says Quetzalcoatl bound us together just before she died. She said we needed each other. Frankly, I kind of wish that she had Chosen someone else."

The admission scandalized Lee. "How can you say that?" she asked, displaying rare passion. "Being Chosen is the grandest thing that can happen to a person. You become part of something bigger and better than yourself. You become something magical!"

"That might have been the case with Quetzalcoatl," Aurora countered, "but it's different with Sadie." She glanced in the youngling's direction. As she did, her expression turned wistful. "Last night, I came face-to-face with the man who burned my home down. He gloated about that, and about his intention to kill Roz. I won't lie. I wanted him dead. For several carpet-bombing moments, I wanted that more than anything I've ever wanted in my life. Sadie picked up on that desire and acted on it. I couldn't stop her. Part of me didn't want to. As a result, that man might be dead."

Lee stared at her, obviously waiting for a punchline. When it did not come, she cocked her head and said, "I do not see the problem. The little one was protecting you. And if the man was here to commit murder, then he got what he deserved."

Naga approved of the sentiment, but she could tell that it did not sit well with Aurora. The woman grimaced, struggling to contain her agitation, and then through gritted teeth, said, "Whether he deserved it or not is irrelevant. The point is: I'm not a killer. I don't want to be a killer. But I'm human, dammit, and bad thoughts cross my mind from time to time. And I'm bound to a dragon who neither has nor understands impulse control. It's not a good fit for me."

Tears welled in her eyes. Seeing that, Roz hurried over and folded her into an embrace. "It's hard at first, Mom," she said, gently rocking her side to side. "But don't worry, you'll get used to it."

"I don't want to get used to it," Aurora said. "I want it to end before someone else gets torn apart because of me."

"Charles brought that end on himself," Roz crooned, still trying to jostle her mother out of her anguish. "In fact, none of this would have happened if not for him."

"Not so," Naga said, having reverted to human form while everyone else was distracted by the emotional mother-daughter exchange. "Tezcatlipoca knows that we stand between him and his goal of claiming the next age. This Charles creature may have been the first to find you, but he was certainly not the only one looking. What happened to the man that Sadie attacked? Did he survive?"

"Answer hazy," Roz said. "I searched all over the neighborhood last night for a body, but didn't find one."

"He could have stumbled into the lake and drowned," Mara said.

Naga pounced on the suggestion. "You are a Seer, yes? Have you had a vision of this?"

Mara flushed, embarrassed to have been singled out by a dragon. "No, no vision," she said sheepishly. "Just a boatload of hope."

"If he had wound up in the water," Roz said, "Brigit would have found him."

"Where is that red-haired wildling anyway?" Max asked, on his way back from the car with a hammer and a roll of duct tape. "I picked up a special bottle of Scotch for her while we were in Sac."

"My best guess is that she's sleeping on the bottom of the lake," Roz said.

"Call her," Naga said. "Tell her to return immediately."

"Nope. Not happening," Roz said, a refusal as cheerful as it was blunt. "She didn't get a lot of time in the water while we were on the road—and she gets really, really cranky when she dries out. She'll be back when she's had a decent soak."

"How long will that take?" Naga asked, bristling at the push-back.

"As long as it takes," Roz replied. "Why? What's the rush?"

"Since no body has been found," Naga said, forcing herself to patience, "we must assume that the second man is still alive. If he is still alive, then he is a threat."

Roz chuckled as if Naga had said something funny. When Naga lifted a lip in warning, she sobered up and said, "I get where you're coming from. And if we were dealing with anyone else, I'd say an overabundance of caution was warranted. However—we're talking about Aldo Whimsey here. He's the biggest idiot on the planet. Trust me. I know."

"Idiot or not," Naga said, "he was here last night. He knows about this place. He will tell or show other agents or drakes where it is. As long as we're still here, that makes him a threat."

"I agree," Aurora said. "In addition to being an idiot, Aldo's mean. He's also obsessed with killing you. That's a combination too dangerous to disregard."

"OK then," Roz said, throwing her hands up in mock-surrender, "we're out of here. But if you don't mind me asking, where are we going?"

"Juarez," Aurora said.

CHAPTER 16

"Juarez."

The word popped out of Aurora's mouth like a bit of chicken bone that had been lodged in the back of her throat. She didn't know why she said it. She'd been thinking of Charles—not mourning exactly, although there was some of that, but with regret for what could have been and what had happened instead. *Sorry about the floor.* Then an old TV screen-shot bubbled up from her memory: a sprawling desert city with a foreboding mountain range imposed on the horizon. She read the caption aloud.

A moment later, she realized that there were eyes upon her.

"What?" she said, a morose return to the here-and-now.

"Why do you say this?" Naga asked.

The gritty image made a second ghostly appearance. This time, it was accompanied by a voice from the past. *'That's the place!'*

"Quetzalcoatl told me that's where we need to go," Aurora said. Shit! That had only been weeks ago? It felt like years. "That's where Tezcatlipoca's lair is."

"When did The Great One tell you this?" Naga asked, waxing suspicious.

"Just before she was attacked. Her Dream-self reached out to me."

"How convenient," Naga jeered, almost but not quite to herself. Louder, she added, "How is it that this is the first time we are hearing of this?"

Aurora took umbrage at Naga's aggrieved tone and so gave it right back to her. "I don't know! Stress does funny things to the memory, and in case you haven't been paying attention, I've had a stressful bunch of weeks. Also, I didn't understand what Quetzalcoatl was trying to tell me until just now."

"It's OK, Mom," Roz said, deliberately stepping between her and Naga. "I think you remembered at just the right time." When Naga indulged in another semi-audible jeer, Roz tipped her head to one side as if she were trying to see something from a different angle and then said, "I think somebody's hungry. Maybe we should continue this conversation after we eat."

Naga understood that she was being teased or even mocked on some level and she was tempted to take offense. But even as she started to huff up, Lee gave her a psychic flick. *"Stop being bitchy and feed."*

"As you wish," Naga said aloud. "You may bring me food."

Lee appeared with a tray piled high with rotisserie chickens and barbecued ribs. As she strode into the living room, Sadie looked up from her mouse-hunt and honked. *"This one, too?"*

"That's for Naga," Aurora told her. *"Your food is in the kitchen."*

Sadie bolted for the kitchen. Everyone else went out to the deck to eat. It was a lovely, late summer morning on the lake. The trees were that gently worn shade of green that precedes the advent of autumn. The water was still and clear. Aurora sat down on the deck's second step with a cup of black coffee. The Marinos flanked her to the left. Roz parked herself to the right. At Roz's nodded invitation, Lee joined them as well.

"Aren't you going to eat, Aurora?" Mara asked, ever the worrier. "There's plenty left—or at least there was a moment ago. If the dragons polished it all off, you can have some of mine."

"Thanks, baby girl," Aurora said, "but I had something on the drive back from the store. And truth be told, I don't have much of an appetite at the moment."

Mara scootched in closer to give Aurora a side hug. "I'm so sorry we weren't here last night. I can't even imagine how horrible that must have been for you."

Aurora patted her con-kid's hand and said, "I'm glad you weren't here. It just would have been two more people in the kill zone."

"Speaking of which," Max said, "are you absolutely sure you want to go to Juarez? It's a pretty rough city. Hundreds of women have gone missing from that area."

"Actually," she said, "it's the mountains to the south of the city that we're interested in."

Max whipped out his cell phone and started typing furiously. As he did so, he cleared his throat once and then again, a time-proven tell that he was distressed. "You're talking about the Sierra Madre Occidentals," he said. "That's a massive range! And it's rated nine point three out of ten on the inhospitable scale. Do we have the right sort of equipment for that kind of expedition? Do we even know where to start looking?"

"I've compared notes with Sadie," Aurora said. "Between her memories of the area and Quetzalcoatl's projection, I think we've come up with a reasonable place to launch our search. And, we don't need equipment. We have dragons.

"But," she went on, in a less business-like tone, "you don't need to worry about any of that, because you and Mara won't be coming with us." A mixture of hurt and relief flashed across Max's face. Aurora was quick to throw his ego a bone. "

Someone needs to handle the tech stuff," she said, and then thanked God when he didn't ask what kind of stuff because she was making this up on the fly. "I'd rather have you do that than climb mountains with your bad knees. And Mara—"

Mara forestalled her with a wink and an upraised hand. "I know. You need me here, too. And I'm quite happy to serve as the rear-guard. If you need something done while you're on the road, I'm on it. If not, I'll keep the home-fires burning." She glanced down at her plate of bones and greasy napkins, then nudged Max with an elbow and added, "Speaking of home, I guess we ought to start packing. Our holiday is over."

"I'll help you," Roz said. "That'll give us a chance to catch up before Brigit gets back."

Their departure left Aurora alone with Lee. Aurora was tempted to take her leave, too, to plead fatigue and go inside for a lie-down. She'd been up until the wee hours scrubbing Charles' blood from the floorboards and just a few hours later, she had roused from a fitful, gore-flecked drowse to drive into town for dragon food and some one-on-one time with Roz. Grabbing some much-needed shut-eye before the next phase of this horror show began seemed like a very good idea. Before she could act on the impulse, though, Lee caught Aurora's eye and said, "I would have a word with you."

The first thought that crossed Aurora's mind was: that's a switch. But the internal filter caught it in time, allowing her to be gracious instead. "Sure," she said. "What's on your mind?"

Lee swallowed hard, a surprising display of discomfort. "I am thinking about your friend. He was not a good man and I am not sorry that he is dead, but I feel sympathy for you for having to watch him die."

"Uhm," Aurora said, unsure of where the conversation was going. "Thank you?"

Lee dismissed the uncertain gratitude aside with a shrug. "I have known trauma. I have suffered loss. I understand—" She stopped suddenly and peered intently into the trees at the base of the deck. The fierceness of her gaze made the hair on the back of Aurora's neck stand straight up.

"What do you see?" she whispered.

"Nothing," Lee replied, not bothering to lower her voice.

"That patch of brush moved, but only for a moment. All is still again."

"Then why are you still staring?"

"Because there is no wind to stir the brush. And brush does not move by itself."

"It could have been a deer," Aurora suggested. "There are plenty of those around here."

"Yes," Lee said, still staring. "It could have been a deer." She broke focus then and stood up in one fluid move. "I think I will see if I can pick up its trail." Almost as an afterthought, she added, "Naga wants to speak to you."

A moment later, she was gone.

Aurora grumbled to herself. Come here. Go there. Naga was one damned bossy drakena. But since refusing a summons from a dragon of her size and temperament could be bad for one's overall health, she crammed her hands in her pockets along with her resentment and headed back into the cottage. Naga was sprawled on the couch, the legs of which had buckled beneath her great weight. The floor all around her was littered with bones.

"Glad to see you're making yourself at home," Aurora said, as she approached. When Naga arched an eyebrow at her, seemingly puzzled by the observation or possibly Aurora's presence, Aurora gave up on trying to be glib and said, "Lee said you wanted to speak with me. What's up?"

Naga's gaze shifted from Aurora to Sadie. The little drakena had dozed off in front of her favorite mouse-hole. The tip of her tail was twitching excitedly, telegraphing a dream hunt. "Do you think her capable of a long and probably arduous journey?"

"Absolutely," Aurora said, "The wound is nothing more than a long scrape—scary-looking but basically harmless."

"It is not the wound that concerns me," Naga said. "She is

defective, is she not?"

Aurora's motherly hackles went up. "What? How do you figure?"

Naga smirked at the question. "There is her size for one thing—"

"That might change over time," Aurora argued. "Even if it doesn't, so what? What does size have to do with anything?"

"Her magical abilities appear to be stunted, too," Naga went on, smirking still as if she were toying with Aurora. "A drakena who cannot disguise herself will have a hard time of moving about in the world of men."

"I'll admit, her human form isn't exactly up to snuff," Aurora said. "She does just fine as a cat, though. And I'm sure as time goes by, she'll learn other shapes."

"You have more confidence in her ability to learn than I do," Naga said. "She seems a bit simple to me."

"Simple?" Aurora echoed, radiating indignation. "You think her simple? I have to say, Naga; you are one judgy dragon."

The accusation did not offend Naga. Indeed, it seemed to stoke the amusement that was seeping out of the corners of her mouth and eyes. "Why do you defend her so fiercely? Did you not wish in front of all of us that she had Chosen someone else?"

The question stripped Aurora's anger away, exposing a thick layer of other emotions that she did not want to own. "I did say that," she granted. "She barges in and out of my head without consideration for my mood or state of mind. She rummages through my thoughts and makes my urges her own. She needs someone stronger than me, someone who can teach her the things that a young, modern drakena needs to know."

An instant after she finished her impromptu admission, embarrassment crept up the sides of her neck and into her cheeks. No wonder Naga despised her! She was weak, a crybaby. You'd never hear Lee whining like that. But instead of damning her with the contempt that she so richly deserved,

Naga favored her with an understanding nod.

"I see now that you do not regret being Chosen by Saidhe," she said. "You just want your bond with her to be more like the one you had with Quetzalcoatl."

Exactly.

Saidhe is new to awareness. You cannot expect mature behavior from her. She is still growing into her psyche."

That made sense!

"Give her time to develop. Give her a chance to learn."

Yes! Little Sadie was still a baby. She needed time!

"Take her someplace safe and leave the hunting to those better suited to it. It will be better that way. Easier."

For one mesmerized microsecond, Aurora found herself agreeing with Naga. It would be better, wouldn't it? Easier, too. Then an internal alarm went off in her head: the damn dragon had tapped into her fatigue and enthralled her! She shook her head, casting off the fascination, and then glared at Naga, who didn't even have the decency to look abashed for having been caught out.

"I get it," she said, trying hard not to snarl. "You think I'm bad luck. Or a magnet for trouble. Who knows? Maybe you're right. But here's the thing. If it weren't for me and that little drakena, you wouldn't even be contemplating a hunt at this point. We've earned our right to be on this expedition."

"Fine," Naga said, shifting from insouciance to an icy glare. "Have it your way. But you are right. I believe misfortune follows you like a hungry dog. It may well be that you will be the ruin of us all."

"I guess we'll just have to see about that," Aurora said, and then walked away, her back as stiff as an upright middle finger.

Aldo spent the night in the Jag. Everything hurt, but oddly enough, only the slashes on his back and chest had bled. The bone-deep bite on his calf had closed up shortly after the attack and was already starting to heal. As he sat there behind the wheel, stinking of stale sweat and clotted blood, he promised himself a hot meal, a warm bed, and a fistful of painkillers when this job came to an end. When pain and fatigue spiked with the dawn, urging him to quit the job and get the hell out of Dodge, he reminded himself that Tezcatlipoca had promised to make him a very rich man.

That kept him going through sunrise. Shortly thereafter, he watched as Roz and Aurora drove away in some POS rental. He thought about following them, but decided to stay put since they hadn't been toting suitcases. An hour or so later, a sleek, golden dragon that looked straight out of Chinatown arrived at the cottage. Aldo gloated to himself: more money in the bank! The Geek Squad turned up next. So, this was where they had been hiding out! Not that it mattered anymore. Then Roz and Aurora came back, hauling what looked to be a half-ton of groceries. Aldo whistled to himself. Feed your lover to a dragon one night, throw a barbecue the next day. Cold, Aurora! Cold!

But the barbecue thing could work to his advantage...

He climbed out of the car and crept back into the woods that hemmed Aurora's property. The best cover he could find was the patch of brush that he had landed in last night. He lowered himself onto his belly, wincing as the gashes in his chest cracked open. He had heard somewhere that big cats didn't hunt in broad daylight, but he had the gun out just in case. Mosquitoes buzzed him as he waited. Ants crawled into his oozing wounds as he watched. Worth it, he told himself, over and over and over again. If this went well, he would never be poor again.

C'mon, c'mon, c'mon!

As if in response to his silent urgings, the cottage door popped open and a mob of people poured onto the deck. Aurora took center stage; her devotees settled down all around her. No one was being particularly loud, but their voices travelled well into the woods.

Then he heard it: "Are you really sure you want to go to Juarez?"

Oh, sweet Jesus! Payday!

More was said, but he barely heard a word. Now that he had what he needed, it was impossible to block out all the other distractions clamoring for his attention: the hard ground and the sharp, dry pine needles poking through his jeans, the Charley-horse in his foot and the brand-new itches screaming to be scratched. He struggled for focus, then abruptly gave up and began to reverse commando-crawl his way back into the woods. As soon as Aurora's cottage was out of sight, he struggled to his feet and made a zombi-esque dash for the Jag. An instant after he hit the driver's seat, he was off and away. Ten miles later, he pulled over and called Tezcatlipoca. The first thing he said when the drake picked up was, "I know where they're going."

When Tezcatlipoca heard, he laughed and laughed.

CHAPTER 18

"Where have you been?"

Drogo Channing scowled, aggravated as much by the question as by the sound of Tezcatlipoca's voice. Why would that rancid old lizard be calling just as he and Azi Zhahhak were returning from their rendezvous with Wo Lung and his Wuhan connection? Did he know what Drogo was plotting? Was he having Drogo watched? Or was his timing just chance? Drogo glanced left and then right, a discreet sweep of the dreary waiting area just outside of baggage claim. All he saw was hordes of baggage-dragging humans, all in a hurry to get on with their miserable lives.

Tezcatlipoca barked at him again. "What's all that noise? Where are you?"

Coincidence then.

Drogo wanted nothing more than to tell the failed god to fuck off, but that bridge wasn't quite ready to be burned yet so he led with a less aggressive counterpunch instead.

"What's it to you?"

"The runaway wyrm is heading to Juarez in the company of two full-grown drakena and some humans," Tezcatlipoca warbled.

The statement astonished Drogo right out of his gameplan. All he could think to say was, "Why?"

"Apparently, they intend to search for my compound."

Drogo's astonishment skyrocketed. Again, all he could say was, "Why?"

To free the other wyrms, of course."

Drogo could not believe that two full-grown drakena would

be that audacious. Or that foolhardy. "How do you know this?" he asked, beginning to shift from surprised to suspicious.

"Carlito's apprentice told me," Tezcatlipoca said, effusive in his glee.

That didn't sound right. Tezcatlipoca didn't talk to human sub-agents. That was his high priest's job. If Carlito wasn't minding the minions, then what was he doing instead—spying, perhaps? Drogo looked over his shoulder again, then lit a cigarette. The rush of nicotine soothed him.

"I thought Carlito was the only one who reported directly to you," he said, trying to sound casual.

"Carlito is dead," Tezcatlipoca said, without a hint of regret in his tone. Not that Drogo would have expected a Great One to mourn such an insignificant loss. That would have been an astounding show of weakness.

"A pity," Drogo said. "I wanted to be the one to kill him." He took another drag and then added, "How did he die?"

"Does it matter?" Tezcatlipoca retorted. "An extraordinary opportunity is heading this way: two, maybe three breeders! If Grishka were here, he would call it a gift from the Divine."

Drogo made a rude noise. "Fucking Grishka. I suppose he has your ear again."

"On the contrary," Tezcatlipoca replied, momentarily less gleeful. "He does not answer his phone. For all I know, he could be dead—or on his way back to Siberia. But who cares? We don't need him anymore."

That was music to Drogo's ears, but scarcely more than a few sour notes. He took a third gusty drag and then said, "So, what do you want of me, Great One? I assume you did not call just to share the good news."

"Indeed," Tezcatlipoca said. "You must come to the compound immediately. Tell your thralls to come, too. The more of us there are on the premises, the easier it will be to subdue the drakena when they arrive. If you do this, I will see that you are the first to breed with one or the other of them."

"A generous offer, Great One," Drogo said, "but I do not think I will be able to muster more than one or two thralls on such short notice. Indeed, I might be the only one available to assist you. Will my presence suffice?"

"I would rather have more," Tezcatlipoca said, "but one is better than none so long as you show up." A moment's pause ensued, an afterthought firing, and then: "You are going to come, aren't you?"

In spite of himself, Drogo had to admire the Great One's instincts. He knew the ground he was treading was treacherous. He just couldn't see where the pitfalls were. "I am finishing up some business here," Drogo said, "so it may take me a day or two to get to you. I will be there, however. That, you can believe."

"Good. Make haste!"

"Of course," Drogo said, but Tezcatlipoca had hung up already so the lie went unheard. He sucked the rest of his cigarette down to the filter, then flicked the expired butt into the road and looked around for Azi Zhahhak. The small, sleek mandrake was stalking a lively group of teenagers who were getting ready to board a charter bus.

"Azi!" he barked. "Time to go."

Azi Zhahhak darkened—a fleeting display of irritation. An instant later, he was standing at Drogo's elbow. "What's the rush?" he asked, still keeping tabs on the teens out of the corner of one eye. "I already have one picked out—the one standing alone and ignored at the far end of the group. I can lure her away while the others are boarding. No one will notice she's gone until it's too late."

Drogo found himself reacting to the mandrake's excited musk. Suddenly, he too craved the thrill of a hunt and that first hot spurt of rich, red blood in the mouth. But even as the urge swept over him, the greater thrill of chasing down destiny reclaimed his attention and he went sober again.

"There's been a change of plans," he said. "We need to get to Juarez."

Azi flushed again and his nostrils widened as if from a stench. "I thought we were done with that old lizard."

We are," Drogo said. "But there are drakena heading toward his compound. He's offered us breeding rights to one of them if we help him subdue them."

That grabbed the whole of Azi's attention in a hurry. He swiveled toward Drogo, his dark eyes alight with a different kind of excitement. His musk turned erotic, too. "A tempting offer!"

"Indeed," Drogo said, breaking into a predatory grin. "But what if we found the drakena before they reached the compound?"

Azi shivered, an orgasmic spasm. "We could take them for ourselves! That would deal a death blow to Tezcatlipoca's manifesto and elevate yours to primacy. The next age would belong to you!"

"Exactly," Drogo crooned. "And," he added, glancing at his expensive window-dressing watch, "if we leave now, we'll have time to hunt while we wait for the drakena to show up."

Naga and Lee left for San Francisco shortly after the barbecue. The drakena claimed that she had to secure her shop in the face of a potentially long shut-down, but Roz wasn't fooled. She knew, as did everyone else, that Naga was unhappy about Aurora being part of the expedition and was making a statement to that effect. In parting, Naga said, "Call me when you reach your resting place tomorrow. We will join you forthwith." *Roz wasn't betting* the farm on that, either.

The following morning, Roz and Aurora ushered their drakena into the bay of a utility van and started on their way. Max and Mara followed them in their Prius until they crossed the Golden Gate Bridge and then parted ways with a toot and a wave.

"I'm so glad they're not coming with us," Aurora murmured, staring out at the city from the passenger window. "I couldn't bear to see either of them get hurt."

"They feel the same way about you, Mom," Roz said, and then settled into the middle lane, intending to follow 101 South all the way into the valley. But Aurora pointed at the exit sign for 280 and said, "Go that way. It's prettier."

Not that she was paying that much attention to the scenery. Thus far, she had spent most of the drive in an uneasy drowse—fretting in her sleep, then starting half-awake with a panicked gasp when her chin hit her chest. Roz had never seen her so out of sorts. This thing with Charles had left her in a bad way—not just the part where he got his admittedly sickening just desserts, but also the part about him seducing and then betraying her. Roz had tried several times to coax her into talking about it, but Aurora could not bring herself to purge.

"Let her be. She's had a shock and needs time ta regroup."

The advice came from the truck's bay. The image that accompanied it was bloody.

"I know," Roz admitted. *"It's just that I hate the thought of her trying to sort through everything that's happened by herself. I'd be a seriously hot mess right about now if that I had been through half of what she has."*

No reply, which either meant that the drakena didn't have an opinion on that or that she had withdrawn to luxuriate in the afterglow that came from an extended stay on a stinky, gooey lake-bottom. Roz was good either way. She was imagining herself in Aurora's shoes, and Aldo in Charles'. No doubt about it. If she had been the one staring down the barrel of her ex-lover's gun, she would've called dragon-fire down on him faster than a thought.

"Pure cac," Brigit noted, gleefully vulgar. *"A offered ta eat that boidheach at least twice an' ye wouldn't have it. More's tha pity, too. Things might have been a lot different if A had."*

"I know," Roz replied, a multi-level admission. But even now, after hearing it straight from her mother's mouth, she could not bring herself to fully believe that Aldo was part of the drake conspiracy. It was so unlike him. He didn't take risks, especially when it came to his own looks or well-being, and he had a knack for disappearing when there was any kind of work to be done. Taking orders didn't exactly suit him, either.

"What I can't figure out is how he and Charles hooked up in the first place."

"Most likely through ewe," Brigit said. When Roz balked at the thought, the drakena pulsed a shrug and added, *"Tha simplest explanation is usually tha one that makes tha most sense."*

Roz scowled, trying to conjure a memory from unyielding fog. If she had introduced Aldo to Charles, she sure as hell couldn't remember doing it. Her thoughts circled back to a faux recollection: Aldo menacing her mother with a goddamn gun. The thought incensed her. *"I really hope he comes after me again,"* she swore. *"If he does, I'll stomp his ass all the way to China."*

"And A'll barbecue tha remains," Brigit added, a thought as casual as it was graphic.

Roz shied away from the visual, choosing instead to lighten up the mood with a joke. "Holy cow!" she said. "Did you just say 'barbecue'? You've been in the states too long. When you get back to Scotland, your friends are going to think you talk funny."

Brigit snorted, a gusty as-if, and then withdrew again.

The van was crossing over the Doran Bridge now. Roz started to point out the iconic Flintstone House to Aurora, but stopped when she realized that her mother was fully asleep. A few moments later, she was glad that she had held off because there it was, a Lexus-sized gap in the passenger side guardrail. "Fuck," she whispered, appalled anew by how close her mother had come to being murdered.

Brigit of course picked up on the feeling. *"Are ye well? Ye felt a wee bit—hungry there fer a moment."*

Hunger had maybe a thousand different meanings to the drakena and Roz was still in the process of categorizing them all. In this case, she guessed that Brigit was referring to the empty feeling that accompanied hunger, a desolate sense similar to loss or near loss. But it was equally possible that she was trying to induce hunger pangs by suggestion. Dragons could be so sneaky!

"It's in our blood," Brigit said, not the least bit apologetic. *"An' dunna think that I dinna notice that ye dinna answer tha question."*

"I'm fine," she replied, trying not to notice the sudden grumbling in her guts. *"Just remembering the good old days when no one was looking to kill us."*

"How good could they have been?" Brigit wondered in reply. *"Ye knew no dragons then."*

"Good point," Roz said, and then smiled. *"You feel like grabbing a snack?"*

They wound up getting drive-through burritos in Palo Alto after stopping to put gas in the van. Aurora slept through that (even though Sadie gulped down a half dozen grande carnitas burritos and bleated for more) and through the beginning of the South Bay's afternoon commuter traffic. Roz inched past exit after familiar exit: Rancho San Antonio, Wolf, Steven's Creek. Nothing seemed to have changed in her absence yet it all felt somehow foreign, as if she had been gone for years instead of months.

Aurora stirred just as the sign for the Saratoga off-ramp spanned into view. "Get off here, honey," she told Roz, her voice still froggy with sleep.

"What?" Roz said, even as she maneuvered the van into a tight space in the right lane. "Why? Where are we going?"

"Home," Aurora murmured in reply. "Just head for home."

Home? What the fuck! Nobody had said anything about going there! An image started to materialize in her head—smoking, ember-eyed ruins highlighted by flashing lights and shouting men. She scowled, trying to pinch the fraudulent memory off, but only succeeded in blocking the lights and the shouting. Shit! She wasn't sure she wanted to confront reality. She wasn't sure she was ready. But if that's what Aurora needed to do, well, then that's what they were going to do.

She took the exit, then drove down another long stretch of road that looked familiar and felt alien. Aurora sat up taller in her seat, but did not seem to come fully awake until Roz turned onto the road that brought them home.

The entryway to the estate was sealed off with slabs of plywood and yellow caution tape. "The fire department must have broken the gate down so they could get to the fire," Aurora said, as she stared at the barrier. "I don't know who boarded the gateway up."

Whoever it was, Roz was grateful to them because the barricade blocked her view of the house. She didn't like being here, not at all. There was a lot of grief floating around, trying to get into her head and make her cry. And now was not the time to grieve for her childhood home and all the memories that had gone up in smoke. Now was the time for clear heads and steady nerves. "So, what's the plan, Mom?" she asked. "Are we going to camp in the pasture tonight?"

"Don't be ridiculous, sweetie," Aurora said. "I just wanted to see the place—you know, to have a moment with your father. We're going to spend the night at Charles' house. It's just down the road from here."

"What?" Was going from burned-down house to dead boyfriend's place a good thing? Or was her poor, overstimulated mother having a moment? "Seriously?"

Aurora shrugged off Roz's concerns. "He's not going to be using it. It's a short trip for Naga and Lee. And no one's going to be looking for us there."

Three reasonable points, Roz decided. Which meant that Aurora wasn't slipping into psychosis! The realization came as such a relief, she let the whole ick factor about crashing the dead boyfriend's pad slide.

"All right then," she said, throwing the van back into gear. "Which way?"

The sun was a shade shy of slipping behind the mountains when Roz took the prescribed turn into Charles' driveway. The marine layer was already pouring into the valley, and while it had yet to fill this particular hollow, its encroaching humidity augmented the ambient smells of redwood tree and equine dung.

"Recognize that Jag?" she asked Aurora, as she cruised toward the end of the driveway.

"Yeah," Aurora said softly, her expression a study in contrasts. "It's his. The pick-up by the shed belongs to him, too. Hmmm. He must've driven up to the lake in a rental."

"Yeah," Roz said. "Probably something big enough to haul a drakena."

An instant after Roz opened the door to the bay, Sadie bounded out. An instant later, she started prancing in place and sniffing wildly at the air. Roz thought she was just happy to be free, but then she and Aurora started communicating. Her mother thought speaking mind-to-mind was rude when there were others around and so addressed the drakena aloud.

"No, that's not horse you're smelling," she said, like a mad woman talking to the wind. "That's zebra. Zebras are meaner and more difficult to kill than horses, and you are recovering from an injury. Perhaps you should try hunting a turkey or deer instead."

More prancing ensued—an urgent, eager dance. *"She is hungry,"* Brigit explained, even as Roz figured that out for herself. *"She wishes tae hunt. A believe A will join her. As A recall, stripy beast is quite toothsome."*

"Sounds good," Roz replied. Then, as an afterthought, she added, *"Before you head off, tell Naga where we are."*

"She knows. She's already on her way," Brigit said distractedly. Then, oozing fog, she headed toward the paddock. With a squawk, Sadie bounded after her.

"Wait!" Aurora said, brow furrowed with concerns.

"It's OK, Mom," Roz said. "Brigit will watch out for her. Let's go inside and split that burrito I picked up earlier. I wish I had thought to buy wine, too. I don't know about you, but I could use a drink."

"Yeah," Aurora said forlornly. "Me, too."

Roz locked arms with her mom and started toward the house. In passing, she tapped the hood of the Jag and said, "Nice ride." Then, as they approached the front door, she said, "I don't suppose he told you where he kept his spare key."

"The door is probably unlocked," Aurora replied, in a faraway voice that matched the look in her eyes. "He wasn't the type to worry about intruders."

Like hell, Roz thought, but to her surprise, Aurora was right. The knob turned; the door swung open. Reflexively, Roz patted the nearest wall down for an entryway switch-plate. Click! Overhead lights winked on, illuminating what looked to be a high-end frat house that had seen one too many parties. The kitchen sinks were heaped with garbage. The counters were littered with trash. And the great room—gross! The carpet was filthy, especially around the massive fireplace. The oversized couch looked as if it had lost a fight with Godzilla.

And what in the name of sweet baby Jesus was that gawd-awful smell?

"Wasn't much for housekeeping, was he?" she asked.

Aurora didn't answer. She was heading toward the fireplace, sleep-walking, it seemed, drawn across the room in spite of herself. There were a few pieces of Native American pottery on the mantle—a curiosity in this Spartan, testosterone-infused atmosphere. The imagery that they bore was primitive yet elegant. Aurora picked up one of the pieces and studied it for a long moment. Then she hugged it to her chest, hung her head, and began to cry.

Roz was mortified. "Mom?" she asked, a tiptoe query. "What is it? What's wrong?"

Aurora wiped her eyes with the back of a forearm and then heaved a sigh laden with regrets. "Charles gave me a piece similar to this," she said. "Brigit told me to ask him where he had gotten it, but I never got around to it. If I had, maybe our house would still be standing. Maybe Quetzalcoatl would still be alive." She set the pot back down on the mantle and buried her face in her hands. "What if all of this is my fault?"

"C'mon, Mom," Roz cajoled, "you know better than that. C'mon," she added, when Aurora remained silent, "let's have some dinner. Your sugar's probably crashing and making you crazy." She headed for the kitchen, hoping to find a clean plate or two in the cupboard. In passing, she saw a wine bottle tucked into a corner by the microwave. The label caught her eye first: Monte Bello: ooh, nice droppa. Then she spotted a familiar number written in an equally familiar hand on the bottom of the label.

"Hey, Mom," she said. "Check this out! He had your number on a wine bottle!"

The oddity didn't jog Aurora out of her funk like Roz had hoped. Indeed, it seemed to deepen her distress. "I gave it to him when we first met," she said, and then covered her mouth with a hand. "I can't believe he kept it! Jesus, why does this have to be so hard?"

The front door banged open, giving them both a start. A moment later, Sadie barged into the house, moving with purpose despite a hugely distended belly. Without so much as a sideways glance at Roz, she barreled over to Aurora and nuzzled her, a gesture both demanding and concerned.

"She wants to know why my heart hurts," Aurora said, as she stroked the drakena's eye ridges. "She wants to know—what?" She started as if stung, and then shifted to scan the surrounds. "She wants to know why this place stinks of drake."

"Shit," Roz said, and set down the unopened bottle of Ridge that she had scavenged from a nearly empty case. "Fresh scent or old?"

"Most likely a combination of both."

The remark came from a hallway that Roz hadn't gotten around to noticing until now. There was a huge man standing at its threshold. The tangles of his unkempt beard were dripping onto his robed potbelly. There were dark rings under his arms, too, as if he had been sweating profusely.

"Aurora," he said, according her a modest bow, "you are a woman of many surprises. I am truly happy to see you alive— and in the company of my little lost one!" He extended a hand in Sadie's direction. "So beautiful you are. Do you remember me?" When Sadie responded with a hiss, he made a comically sad face and said, "Is that any way to greet the one who saved your life?" He stretched forth his hand again. "Come, little one. You need not be afraid. Your djadja will not hurt you."

"She may be little," Aurora said, placing herself between the two dragons, "but she's not stupid. She knows what drakes do to drakena. She was there the night Quetzalcoatl was killed."

Grishka bristled. His agitation made him seem oddly fluffy. "That travesty," he snarled, "was none of my doing. They were only supposed to subdue her. So much knowledge—lost. So much history, wasted. You must believe me, little one," he said, speaking directly to Sadie, 'that was not the end your djadja desired for the Great One."

Sadie hissed again and sank into a tail -thrashing crouch. As she prepared to launch herself at Grishka, Brigit ambled into the house radiating well-fed contentment. She spotted Sadie first. Then, as her gaze shifted to Grishka, Roz experienced a pang of loathing that turned suddenly and astonishingly erotic. Brigit snorted as if trying to expel the drake's musk from her nostrils and then very carefully backtracked toward the door. As she did so, she shared a thought with Roz. "*Feck! A canna be in tha same room with that one!*"

"Great," Roz replied, even though she wanted desperately to be downwind of the drakena's throbbing libido. *"What if I need you?"*

"A will be listening. If there is need, A will come."

With that, the drakena was gone.

"I remember you now," Grishka said, wagging a gnarled forefinger at Roz. "We met on a cruise ship out of Glasgow. You said you wanted to be alone because you were recovering from a broken heart. You were really waiting for that drakena, weren't you?" When Roz declined to answer, he returned his attention to Aurora. Casually, as if they were old friends, he said, "You keep remarkable company."

"You know how it goes. The end of an age makes for strange bedfellows," she quipped drily.

"You have no idea," he replied, and then ran his fingers through his soggy beard. "But where are my manners? Please! Sit down! We have much to discuss and talking is always more pleasant in a semi-folded position. You will forgive the abundant disorder. Cleanliness is not a habit that dragons entertain."

Roz snorted, a silent you-can-say-that-again. Brigit responded with the mental equivalent of a flick.

"Will you drink?" Grishka went on, ignoring the fact that none of his would-be guests had moved. "Yes, we are all friends here. Let us drink! I have vodka. Or, if you prefer, Carlito has wine—" He paused, taken by a thought, then scowled like a baby with gas and said, "You are not here to see him, are you? Because he is not here. I believe—" He trained his shaggy gaze on Roz. "I believe he was searching for you. You are Aurora's daughter, are you not?"

Again, Roz refused to either confirm or deny. Brigit approved of her taciturnity. *"Dunna give him anything he can use."*

He sighed, an internal surrender of sorts, then pulled a bottle of vodka out of a mostly full case and cracked it out with one easy twist. "Na zdorovie!" He took a long glug from the bottle, then shuffled over to the dilapidated couch and threw himself onto it. The frame let out a wooden groan, one that he had no doubt heard before.

"So," he said, after another pull, "what are you doing here? Have you come in search of Carlito?" He eyed her slyly for a moment, and then added, "No, I do not believe that is why you are here.""

Aurora sucked in a traumatized breath, and for a moment, Roz feared that her mother was going to spill the entire pot of beans. "Believe what you will. Our business is our own."

He gave his head a sorry shake, then swigged again from the bottle as if to rinse a sour taste from his mouth. "Ah. Such mistrust. Please know that I do not blame you. If our situations were reversed, I might feel the same. I swear by the Divine that I mean you no harm. Moreover, I wish to make amends. Ask me anything. I will speak nothing but truth."

"Why?" That was Brigit, speaking through Roz. This was the first time that the drakena had used her as a mouthpiece and Roz had to say, she didn't much care for the sensation. "Such is nae the way of yer kind."

Grishka eyed her slyly, as if he knew exactly who was doing the talking. "It is true," he said. "Most drakes are creatures of instinct, selfish and uninterested in change. And look where that's gotten us: isolated, in hiding, driven by desperation to diabolical schemes. I tried with all my might to persuade Tezcatlipoca to spare Quetzalcoatl. The Divine wanted her to live out her time in peace. But neither the Great One nor his rival Drogo Channing could bring themselves to rise above their natures and evolve. Instead, they killed one of the Divine's first-borns. For that, I repudiate their conspiracy. From this moment on, I side with you."

The house went outer-space quiet, which made the waves of astonishment and doubt that were battering Roz's psyche feel ten times stronger. She snuck a peek at Aurora. Both her brow and her mouth were puckered, as if she had swallowed something foul and could not decide if it would be better to choke it down or spit it out. Her dragon was curled up on the floor behind her, bulging belly protected by her tail. Her eyes were closed, but Roz could tell that she was spying rather than sleeping.

"Go on," Grishka urged. "Ask me anything."

Brigit was the first to cast her vote. *"As long as he's taking requests, ask him ta feck off and go away."*

But Aurora spoke up first. "Where is Tezcatlipoca keeping the wyrms?" she asked. "Why does he want them?"

His response was immediate. "He has them confined to his compound in the mountains beyond Juarez. They were given high doses of hormone to influence the direction of their sexing. Those that sex female will be used as breeding stock. Those that sex male will be culled."

"How many of them are there?" Aurora asked. "How many of them have sexed?"

"Wrong questions," Brigit remarked, sotto voce like a golf commentator.

"There are twenty-five wyrms in all," the drake replied conversationally, "not including yonder youngling and the one who escaped with her. Half of them were in the process of sexing when last I saw them. By now, I imagine all of them are in some stage of transition. That should make it easier for you to rescue them."

"What?" Roz blurted. An instant later, the presence in her head took a sudden chill. *"He knows nothing. Tell him nothing."*

Grishka snorted as if he had heard the thought. "You think I am fishing. How quaint. Yet you tell me much without even speaking. Aurora and the little one are bonded, so you must have some sense of where Tezcatlipoca's compound is located. And you must foil the Great One if you wish to secure the next age. How better to do that than to hijack the ones who are essential to his plan?"

Brigit huffed—grudging admiration. *"His back may be twisted, but his wit is as robust as his smell. A definitely have tae keep away from him."*

"You know too much," Aurora said. "Tell me why we shouldn't kill you."

The drake shrugged, an awkward show of insouciance. "Kill me if you must; I will not resist. But you would do better to use me as a guide. I know the exact location of Tezcatlipoca's compound. I know where he houses the wyrms."

Aurora brightened at that and glanced at Sadie, who was now snoozing. To Roz, she said, "If we took him along, we could leave Sadie here, safe from danger."

"Oh no," Rasputin said. "That won't do. The little one needs to come with us. We may have need of her.!"

A thunderous roar erupted outside. *"Naga's here,"* Brigit remarked, with the equivalent of an eyeroll. *"She wants ta know what we're doing in tha company of a drake. Mercy, tha fuss she's raising. So—dramatic."*

Roz suppressed a snicker. Although neither of them was in on the conversation, both Aurora and Grishka obviously knew what was going on outside and why. Aurora bit her lower lip and scowled while Grishka looked positively delighted.

"There are more of you?" he warbled. "I am impressed. Truly. Tezcatlipoca will not be able to withstand you in such numbers. How splendid!" He slugged back a draught of vodka and then added, "Will the new arrivals come in and accept hospitality? Or should I go to them?"

"Tell him ta stay put," Brigit said, and while Roz couldn't be sure, she thought she sensed a hint of possessiveness in the drakena's subconscious. *"Naga's already threatened ta kill him. A have to keep on reminding her tha we're drakena, not drakes. Hang on, A'm goin' ta try and fill her in on what's been said so far."*

"Your invitation of hospitality has been declined," Roz told Grishka. "And if you venture outside at this point, this might well be your last night on earth."

Grishka shrugged. "I placed my life in the Divine's hands long ago, child. If She wishes me dead, it will happen. If She does not, I will survive. Still," he added, helping himself to more vodka, "pain that serves no purpose is counterproductive. I believe I will remain where I am."

Another roar sounded outside, louder and more vociferous than the first. It was followed by a muffled whoosh and then a flurry of driveway grit and gravel hitting the front door. An instant later, Brigit broke the news.

"Her highness has left in a royal snit. In parting, she offers this advice. Do not trust tha drake. Do not travel with him. If he betrays you, and he surely will, I willna come tae your aid."

"Is there a problem?" Rasputin asked, with exaggerated nonchalance.

"No," Roz said. "Not at all."

CHAPTER 20

Aurora and her daughter left with their drakena just as the night was getting interesting. They would not tell Grishka where they were going, only where he could meet them in Mexico. He was sorry to see them go. He would have enjoyed some companionship on the long, boring trip to Juarez. Oh, he understood their reasons. The water drakena found him too attractive for comfort. And the little one despised him for the upbringing that he had inflicted on her. So sad. Even human company would have sufficed. Strong, quick-witted women like Roz had appealed to him since the days of the tsarina. He found Aurora compelling as well even though she'd been rather distracted. It was to be expected given the circumstances, he supposed. Even so, he would have liked the chance to charm her into a better mood.

But no. They were cautious, and rightly so. Only a fool relied on trust at the end of an age.

The bottle that he had opened to celebrate their arrival was empty now. He slung it aside, ignoring the ensuing crash, then heaved to his feet and went to the door for a breath of evening air. The giant, shaggy-barked trees that surrounded Carlito's lair were barely visible through the fog, but their earthy fragrance hung in the mist like the Divine's perfume. There were no trees like these in Russia. He'd miss them when he finally returned to his territory. He closed his eyes, trying to imagine that day, but the Divine would not grant him that vision.

"I can't believe you just let them go."

Grishka's wistful mood took a sour turn. He inhaled deeply, savoring the tree-spiced air one last time, and then, without turning around, said, "I believe I told you to remain hidden until I gave you the all clear."

"You would have left me in that pool shed all night," Aldo groused. Which was probably not far from the truth. "Do you have any idea how hard it is to breath in a place where chlorine is stored?"

"If a dragon can't smell you," Grishka said blandly, "a dragon won't eat you."

Aldo jeered. "Next time, just wrap me in Saran Wrap."

"You should be careful what you ask for," Grishka said, and then half-turned to stare down at Carlito's former apprentice. His clothes were disheveled. He reeked of chlorine and unwashed body. His scabrous wounds were cracked in places. What had Carlito seen in this train-wreck of a man? "What is your interest in them anyway?"

"Tezcatlipoca is paying me for information about the dragons," Aldo said. "And I've got a score to settle with Roz."

Grishka's eyebrows leapt up like startled caterpillars. "Really? How do you know her?"

"We were together up until a few months ago," Aldo said, bragging in a contemptuous sort of way. "I broke it off with her on a trip to Scotland. She was just too self-centered for me."

"I see," Grishka said, even as his eyes narrowed. "And what kind of information will the Great One be paying for tonight?"

"Just that at least two she-dragons are on their way," Aldo said, and then cast Grishka a look that was both hopeful and wheedling. "You wouldn't happen to know what happened to the third one, would you? He's going to ask."

"I could tell you," Grishka replied, thoughtfully stroking the tangles of his beard, "but that's not the news he going to want to hear."

"Oh, really?" The hope in his expression hardened into greed. "I'm all ears, dude."

"Get your phone," Grishka said, and just like that, the phone was in Aldo's hand. "Text Tezcatlipoca this: 'Two drakena are heading south. Grishka is with them and means to deliver them unto you.'"

Aldo looked up from his texting to gape at Grishka. "Seriously, dude? You're going to turn them over? The women, too?" When Grishka nodded, the human lit up like a Broadway theater marquee. "Oh my God, that's fucking awesome! I wanna be there to see that!" He put a hand on Grishka as if they were great friends and added, "You have to let me come with you!"

Grishka removed the offending hand with exaggerated gentleness, as if it were a kitten that had lost its way. "There are risks involved," he said, "and you are injured. It would be best if you stayed here and focused on your recovery."

Aldo folded his arms across his chest and scowled like a child who was getting ready to throw a fit. "What exactly am I supposed to do here while I'm recovering?" Aldo groused. "This place is so far out in the sticks, it doesn't even have pizza delivery."

"The internet here is quite good," Grishka said. "Go to Amazon and order anything you want. Charles isn't going to mind, is he?"

"Wait," Aldo said, looking dumfounded. "Dragons use the internet?"

"Smart ones do," Grishka replied.

Aldo laughed, and then bobbed his head several times as if he were following a bouncing ball. Then he said, "Seriously, dude, you're going to need me. How else are you going to be able to deliver that many live-and-kicking bodies to Mr. T?"

The sheer audacity of the man, reducing the former god of magic and death to a single initial with an empty honorific in front of it! Tezcatlipoca would have had the man's heart on a platter for such a show of disrespect and Grishka would have been content to watch. Even so, he drew his mouth into a semblance of a smile and winked. "That is the beauty of my plan," he said. "They offer me no resistance. You may share that with Tezcatlipoca as well."

"Oh my God," Aldo said, as he tapped at his phone, "this is so great. You have to let me go with you, Grish. You just have to! If you don't—" He paused. Sly lights danced into his eyes. "If you don't, I'll tell Tezcatlipoca that you're—" His brow knitted as he were trying to dredge up the perfect impetus. "I'll tell him that you and Charles were scheming against him."

Grishka shrugged. "The Great One was a god. He can taste a lie before it leaves your lips."

Aldo stomped his foot. "C'mon, dude. You gotta let me do this."

Grishka stared at him for a long moment, weighing his options. Then, decided, he nodded as if persuaded and made himself look friendly again. "Did you finish your message?" he asked. When Aldo held the phone out for Grishka to see, he snatched it up in one gnarled hand and read the text. Then, for good measure, he scrolled through earlier parts of the thread. There were no other mentions of him. Good. A lie was more believable if it was built on the back of fact. He made a fist, crushing the phone. Aldo let out a yelp and then gaped at the mangled ruins that Grishka let fall to the floor.

"What the fuck, dude?" he gabbled. "That was my phone!"

"It's called controlling the flow of information," Grishka said matter-of-factly. "But don't worry. You're not going to be needing it."

"But—!"

Grishka grabbed Aldo by the throat and pulled his face close so he could see the fire that was rising up for him. Aldo struggled to free himself, but could not escape Grishka's unyielding grip. "I don't understand," he gasped, as Grishka lifted him off his feet by his jaw-bones. "I—I thought we had an—understanding."

"If you had understood anything at all," Grishka said, squeezing off Aldo's airway bit by inexorable bit, "you would not have tried to blackmail a dragon."

CHAPTER 21

Aurora stood in line at the TSA checkpoint, trying not to fidget as sweat trickled down her spine and her socks grew damp. She wasn't worried for herself. She had proper ID. So did Roz. Brigit, however, was traveling with Mara's passport. "Sure," she'd said, when Roz asked Mara to overnight the ID to the motel where they had relocated for the night. "Anything for the cause. But," she added, looking chagrined, "we don't look anything alike!"

"Brigit can make—adjustments," Roz had replied. "Leastwise, enough to clear security."

"If you say so," Mara said, in that tiptoe tone that some people take with growling dogs and crazies. Now, from her vantage point three bodies behind Roz and the changeling, Aurora could see all too well that Mara's apprehension was justified. Brigit's version of Mara was too tall. Too robust. Too red-headed ('Some things just canna be changed!'). The TSA agent was going to spot the discrepancies immediately and then all hell was going to break loose. There would be handcuffs. A struggle. Guns drawn and—

"Hey, lady!" a male voice to her rear barked. "Move it! You're holding up the line!"

Crap! Roz and Brigit were already handing their documents to the agent! Roz made some comment—a joke possibly. The agent's only response was to return her documents and wave her toward the line for the body scanner. Then he turned his attention to Brigit, glancing from her to the passport and back again, scowling the whole time. Aurora started looking around for possible distractions only to be chastised by the guy behind her again.

"Jesus, lady! Pay attention!"

Brigit was already on her way to join Roz.

Oh, thank God!

They all regrouped at their departure gate, Roz with a bagful of breakfast sandwiches and Brigit with a red Solo cup filled almost to the rim with what smelled like whiskey. When Aurora arched a dubious eyebrow at the changeling, she shrugged and said, "This is my first time on an aeroplane. A feel tha need fer fortification."

"You want one of these, Mom?" Roz said, reaching blindly into the bag. "If so, you'd better grab one now. They're going to be gone in a minute."

"No, thank you," Aurora said, still too on edge to eat. "I'll get a box on the—"

"It's cold in here!" The thought hit her psyche like a cannonball, displacing everything in its way. *"It smells like dog, too, and there is no room for getting comfortable!"*

"I told you this wasn't going to be pleasant," Aurora replied, trying not to feel guilty for having arranged for Sadie to travel in the cargo hold as an exotic cat. *"But it was the only way I could get you on this plane."*

"You should have let this one fly," Sadie sulked. *"This one knows the way."*

"It would have taken you weeks to get where we need to go. This way will take less than a day."

An icy sniff ensued. *"This one should have left with Naga. Naga is no fun, but she would not have stuffed this one into a dark, smelly container."*

"I wouldn't be so sure of that," Aurora replied dryly. *"Besides, Naga did not invite you to go with her. Naga doesn't want anything*

to do with any of us." Because of Grishka. Or maybe her. Or possibly both. Aurora wasn't surprised that the drakena had found an excuse to bow out of the expedition, but she had to admit, it was disappointing.

"Djadja then," Sadie said, perversely persistent. *"He would have taken this one with him."*

"Yes," Aurora replied, *"I suppose he would have. But if he had asked, would you have gone?"*

Aurora felt the youngling lunge toward an affirmation only to pull herself back at the last moment. *"No,"* she said instead. *"He hurt this one before when this one did not conform to his desires. Who is to say that he would not do so again?"*

"Good point," Aurora said, and then skidded to a full mental stop as a dissonant thought struck her. *"But—didn't you feel drawn to him? I thought drake musk was like catnip to drakena at this stage of an age."*

"This one does not understand what you just said," Sadie replied. *"Djadja smelled as he always has to this one."*

Interesting, Aurora mused, and then lost her train of thought as the PA crackled. "Flight 1362 for El Paso, Texas is now ready for pre-boarding. First class passengers—"

"We're being loaded onto the plane," Aurora said. *"I need to focus on that for a while. I'll rejoin you when we're in the air. Get some sleep if you can."*

Sadie responded with another sniff. *"Sleep is unlikely. The smell of dog is making this one hungry!"*

"Try anyway," Aurora said, and then returned to the here-and-now to find both Roz and Brigit grinning at her. "What?" she demanded, more defensively than she'd intended.

"I recognize that face," Roz said gleefully. "You used to make it all the time when I was a teenager—usually when I was bugging you. My guess is that you've been communing with Sadie."

"Bingo," Aurora said, pinching the bridge of her nose in hopes of blocking the headache that was trying to invade the space behind her eyes. "She's not happy about being in the hold." She massaged the center of her forehead for a moment, and then added, "I know the situation isn't ideal, but I did the best I could for all of us."

Roz gave her a hug, trying to squeeze her into a better mood. "Of course you did, Mom. And don't worry about Sadie. She's going to be just fine."

"You think?" Aurora asked, desperate for affirmation.

"She'll be fine," Brigit said, as she glugged the last of her drink. "Ye'll see. We drakena are wondrously resilient."

Grishka was being watched.

Whoever it was was very good at not being seen. He had only caught a single glimpse of his stalker—one furtive, out-of-place movement out of the corner of an eye, there and gone again so quickly that someone less attentive might have mistaken it for a trick of the eye. But Grishka was not easily fooled; his eyes were guided by the Divine. Someone at this train station was watching him.

The realization came as no great surprise. Tezcatlipoca had eyes everywhere. And The Great One would definitely be looking for Grishka after receiving that baited text from the late, not-so-great Aldo Whimsey. Grishka still could not believe that that preening clod had survived a drakena ambush when Carlito had not. In a way, it made his failure to survive Grishka's ambush that much sweeter.

His gaze strayed from shadow to shadow—a casual, almost playful attempt to discern his stalker's identity. One thing was sure: it wasn't Drogo. That unevolved *yascheritsa* would have been breathing fire in Grishka's face by now. It wasn't any of Drogo's thralls, either. None of them had the right temperament for spying. Indeed, the only one who might have been able to tail Grishka without getting caught was Carlito. Alas. Grishka would miss the man, even if The Great One didn't.

An announcement blared over the PA: his train was now boarding. He heaved to his feet like an old man would and shuffled his way toward the platform. He didn't check to see if he was being followed because it didn't matter, really. At the

Divine-appointed time, his shadow would be revealed to him and he would proceed from there. In the meantime, all he needed to do was bide his time.

CHAPTER 23

Drogo Channing was trailing after a young factory worker who was late getting home from the maquilladoras when his phone rang. She glanced nervously over her shoulder. Drogo took the call, thinking that doing so would give his prey a false sense of security.

"Where are you?"

Tezcatlipoca. Again. He mostly suppressed a disgusted grunt and said, "What is it now?"

"Grishka has surfaced."

The news irritated Drogo. He had not expected Rasputin to reappear after staying quiet for so long. The cripple was in Tezcatlipoca's cross-hairs at the moment, but he had an uncanny knack for worming his way out of a tight spot. A reconciliation between the two could screw up Drogo's plans.

"So what?" he asked, feigning disinterest.

"He's with the drakena," Tezcatlipoca crooned. "He's bringing them to me."

That stopped Drogo in his tracks. "Grishka's no match for a wyrm, never mind a pack of full-grown drakena. There's no way he could keep them all under control."

"He does have unnatural powers of persuasion," Tezcatlipoca pointed out. "It could be that he also has some other kind of magic that he has kept to himself. All I know for sure is that the drakena are with him and that he is bringing them to me."

"I don't believe it," Drogo snarled. "Rasputin is lying to you."

"I did not hear this from Grishka," the Great One said. "One of my spies contacted me with the news."

"I still don't believe it," Drogo said.

"You are welcome to your disbelief," Tezcatlipoca said flatly. "I just called to let you know that I won't be needing you or your thralls here at the compound after all. Grishka alone will suffice."

Shit! The situation was worse than Drogo had imagined! Grishka hadn't even shown his filthy hirsute face yet and he was already back in Tezcatlipoca's good graces. Drogo had to slow this runaway reunion down and then crash it!

"If I were you," he said, "I would not be so quick to trust Rasputin again. If he had such exciting news, why did he not tell you of it? Why has he not answered your calls?"

"Excellent questions. I will ask them when he gets here."

Instinct surged within Drogo, primal recognition of a straw ready to be grasped. "I think I should be there when you question him," he said. "In fact, I think I should intercept him and then accompany him and the drakena to your compound."

"Why would you do that?" Tezcatlipoca asked, arching his tone as if it were his neck. "Your despite for Grishka knows no limit."

"It's true," Drogo admitted. "I harbor nothing but loathing for that twisted ruin of a drake. I also question his motives. I offer to do this simply to make sure he delivers on his promises."

Tezcatlipoca went silent: the rancid old lizard weighing his options. A moment later, he cleared his throat and said, "I agree. A degree of caution is warranted. He is heading for Juarez. He travels by train. Call me when you find him."

The line went dead. Drogo slipped the phone into a pocket and then lit a cigarette. The nicotine tingled through his veins along with a new strain of excitement. Not only was he going to whisk the drakena out from under Tezcatlipoca's nose, he was going to exterminate his chief counselor, too!

What a glorious outing this was shaping up to be!

Now, where did that little factory creature get to?

CHAPTER 24

I have concerns," Lee said. *"This does not feel right."*

"You are being emotional," Naga said, projecting a coolness that she did not entirely feel. *"This needs to be done."*

"We should be with the others," Lee insisted. *"They could be in danger."*

"I know. That is why this needs to be done."

CHAPTER 25

As the airplane began its descent into the El Paso borderplex, the cloud cover dissipated, offering Aurora her first glimpse of El Paso. It was a sprawling desert metropolis, miles upon miles of parched brown basin overlaid with haze. A smattering of high-rises marked its center while a rugged dragon's tail of a mountain range crowned the horizon. As she studied the city, searching in vain for a glimpse of the Rio Grande, the plane hit a pocket of thermal turbulence and shuddered violently. From across the aisle, she heard Roz whisper, "Steady, Bridge, we're almost there. At the same time, Sadie erupted for what had to have been the thousandth time.

"This one hates human-flight!" she raged. *"This one wants out now!"*

"Soon," Aurora promised, knowing full well that it would not be anywhere near soon enough.

The drakena continued her tirade throughout the descent. Aurora tried to shut the raging out, but she was bone-tired and her guard kept slipping. By the time the plane finally landed, she was a hair away from screaming. She wasn't the only one in distress, either. Brigit was as tight-lipped and pale as Aurora had ever seen her, and her arm-rest had finger-shaped dents in it. An instant after the plane touched down, she lunged to her feet and lurched toward the exit. When their southern-belle of a flight attendant came steaming toward her, intent on ordering her back into her seat, Roz warned her off.

"I wouldn't if I were you."

The warning alone might not have done the trick, but

166

coupled with the threat display that Brigit was rocking, it had the desired effect. The flight attendant backed off with a weary, "Bless your heart," and Brigit was the first one off the airbus.

"Last feckin' time A do that," she said, as Roz and Aurora joined her on the ground. Neither mother nor daughter tried to talk her out of that decision.

They found Sadie's crate in an out-of-the-way corner of the cargo area. It was bucking and shaking like an unbalanced washing machine. "What all do you have in there?" the baggage handler asked, when Aurora presented him with her paperwork. "A lion?"

"I wish," Aurora replied, and then winced as Sadie blasted her with a thought. *"This one wants out! Now!"*

"Soon," she said, a weary reflex by now. *"We have to get to the motel first."*

The crate jumped and shuddered with extra vehemence. *"No! No more 'soon'!"*

The baggage handler flung a receipt at Aurora and cleared out. *"Now!"*

Aurora slumped, defeated by the drakena's seemingly boundless energy. She couldn't let her out in such a public place; she'd attract too much attention in enemy territory. But there was no reasoning with her, either. She had release on the brain and nothing else would suffice. As she stressed over her next move, Brigit stepped up to the still bucking crate and gave it a solid thump with her fist. At the same time, she broadcast an empathic command.

"Calm yerself!"

The crate went still, but Sadie remained agitated. *"You don't understand! It is stifling in here! This one cannot breathe!"*

"Dunna be silly. Yer uncomfortable, nuthin' more. Tha's nae reason tae make tha rest of us suffer."

"*But—*"

"*But nuthin'. Yer a dragon, not some brainless beast. Endure what must be endured from a place of strength and self-control. Trust tha we willna make ye stay in there any longer than we have tae.*"

Sadie huffed, sullen acquiescence. But her mood remained a seething black cloud all the way to the motel where they were to rendezvous with Grishka. As soon as they filed into their deluxe casita and closed the door, Aurora opened the crate. "There," she said, as the drakena burst into view. "That wasn't so bad. Was it?"

Sadie shuddered, offloading stress, and then scorned Aurora with a narrow-eyed look. "*You are no better than Djadja.*"

Being compared to a hairy, hunch-backed drake did not sit with Aurora, especially not after all the grief that this little shit of a dragon had given her today. She huffed up with affront and said, "How do you figure?"

"*You kept this one captive!*"

Aurora was quick to correct her. "I transported you," she said. "When we reached the place where we needed to be, I released you. There's a difference. Surely you see that."

The drakena rustled her iridescent wings, an impudent refusal to see reason. "*You kept this one captive.*"

"Fine," Aurora said, too tired to pursue the argument further, "have it your way. Let me make it up to you. Are you hungry? I'll call out for something. Anything you want."

Sadie hissed. "*This one is done with being treated like a pet. This one is going hunting.*"

The declaration shocked Aurora out of her pique and into full-on maternal mode. "That's not a good idea! It's dark out. You don't know the area. You could get lost—"

Sadie cut her off with another hiss. "*This one is a dragon. Dragons do not get lost!*"

"But—"

"This one will come and go as this one pleases, just like you."
Aurora cocked her head at Brigit, inviting her to intervene again. The changeling refused the offer with a shake of her head. "As long as she does nae let herself be seen, A see no harm in her spreading her wings."

Ugh. Dragons. There was just no reasoning with them. And, at least for tonight, Aurora was done trying. Fine," she said, and strode over to the sliding glass door that led to the terraza. "Come and go via the patio," she said, ordering, not asking. "See you whenever."

Sadie snorted at her in passing and then disappeared into the night. Kids these days, she thought and then started to slide the door shut only to be forestalled by Brigit. Aurora blinked back a moment's surprise, and then came to a reassuring conclusion."

Oh, thank God," she said. "You're going with her."

Brigit reared back as if in disbelief. "Dunna be daft, woman. A'm off tae find water. A need a serious soak tae settle myself after being so far from tha ground fer so long. A dunna know how you humans tolerate such flight. Tis feckin' unnatural!"

With that, she too disappeared into the night.

"Is it just me," Aurora said, as she drew the slider shut, "or can overexposure to dragons cause headaches?"

Roz laughed. "It's not just you. Bridge was so stressed about cruising at 30,000 feet, she damn near made my head explode. Not only that, I'm covered with dragon sweat. I need to jump into the shower before I wind up peeling skin off along with my clothes. And if I want to salvage my jeans, I'll have to hit a laundromat afterward. You want to come with? We can grab a bite while we're out."

"Thanks," Aurora said, "but dealing with my bratty counterpart has left me knackered. I'm going to lie down and hopefully get some shut-eye."

As soon as the words left her mouth, a wave of weariness crashed over her, leaving her unsteady on her feet. She kicked off her tennis shoes one after the other, then flopped down on the nearest of the two beds and dragged a pillow over her head. The pillowcase was soft to the touch and smelled of starchy air-conditioning. The combination swept her away to a hotel room from her past, the one where she and Charles had spent that one amazing night. She sighed into the pillow, remembering his touch, the passion, their incredible compatibility. Then she remembered everything else and choked back a sob that doubled as a curse.

Bastard!

Getting played was a hard enough pill to swallow. Getting played by a murderer turned that pill into a time-bomb that kept on going off in her head. He had killed Quetzalcoatl. He had meant to kill Roz. And—damn it! He had been ready to kill her. How did one wrap one's head around the contradiction? How could she have not seen through the Captain Fantastic facade and spotted the ugliness lurking within? How could he have hidden his dark side so well?

She tried to console herself. Again.

It wasn't her fault that she'd fallen for him.

It wasn't her fault that he'd hunted her down.

And—it wasn't her fault that he was now dead.

An image took shape in her mind: him tucked away in some dark underwater notch, his landscaped veneer all blue and bloated, his hair waving at the surface like turtle grass. She had nothing on which to base the image. Brigit hadn't shared her thoughts with Roz when she finally returned from the lake— or if she had, Roz hadn't shared them with Aurora. She just knew that that was how he'd ended up. His fate offered her no comfort. But if God Himself offered her the chance to go back in time and engineer a different outcome, she wasn't sure that she'd sign on.

Did that make her a bad person?

She was drowsing now, surfing that hazy grey space between sleep and consciousness. She felt restless; windswept. Her dreams were chaotic—flash-bang glimpses of past and future, memory emulsified with inference. A pink-frilled dragon sashayed out of the ether. Esmerelda! Aurora's dream-heart swelled with affection and rue. How she missed those days, the innocent adventures, happy endings. She and Ezzie spiraled through time and space, a dizzying tailspin that came to an end on a rooftop overlooking the moonlit outskirts of an afterhours shantytown. A pair of coydogs trotted down the hardscrabble main drag, trailing after something that Aurora could not see. As her dream-self strained for a clarifying glimpse, the ether reddened, taking on the colors of fire and blood. A wave of urgency crashed into her, washing her back onto the grainy shores of wakefulness.

An instant later, the patio door rattled as if in the grips of an earthquake. It took Aurora a moment to remember that she was in Texas, not California.

The door rattled again. *"Let this one in!"*

Still groggy from her abrupt awakening, it didn't occur to Aurora to wonder why Sadie was back so soon until the drakena shoved past her as she opened the door and hissed, *"Shut it shut it shut it!"*

Aurora did so. Then, seeing how wild-eyed and trembly the youngling was, she drew the blinds as well. *"What's wrong?"*

"We should leave this place," Sadie replied, refusing to meet Aurora's gaze. Her nostrils were white around the rims, a sure sign of stress. *"We should leave now."*

"Why?"

"It may be that this one has been compromised."

Aurora's heart plunged toward her colon. The sensation left her dizzy, and she struggled to keep her ensuing thought steady.

"How?"

"This one went into the desert to hunt for bouncy long-ears," Sadie said, projecting the image of a rabbit. *"They make their lairs in sand hills and only come out after dark. As this one was stalking one in its hole, a human female passed nearby, running hard and stinking of fear. A short time later, a pair of large dogs came sniffing after her at a leisurely pace, as if they were driven by something other than appetite. This one was happy to leave them to their hunt, but even as they trotted off into the darkness, the larger of them skidded to a stop and looked in this one's direction. As soon as we made eye-contact, this one sensed the drake within the dog. This one bolted. This one is skilled at evasion. But—"* She rustled her wings and swallowed hard. *"This one is not sure if she lost the drake.*

"We should go."

Shit.

Aurora was in motion in an instant, making a to-do list in her head as she grabbed her phone and purse. As soon as they got clear of this place, she'd have to call Roz and tell her to stay away. She'd have to contact Grishka, too. After that—

The front door deadbolt snapped back. The door started to open. Sadie thrust herself in front of Aurora and sucked in an oversized breath, getting ready to flame whoever crossed that threshold. As she did so, Aurora forestalled her with a thought.

"I don't think drakes would bother with a key."

A pizza box appeared in the gap between door and jamb. An instant later, Roz stepped into view. The smile on her face collapsed when she saw Sadie shielding Aurora and ready to attack. "What's going—on?"

The last word burst out of her, propelled by a forceful push from behind. She pitched forward. The pizza box sailed through the air, somersaulting once before hitting the floor and ejecting its contents onto the catfood-colored tiles. Roz pivoted, fists balled, sputtering, "What the—" only to be shouldered further into the room by a hulking torpedo of a mandrake. He was muscular and bald, with cold grey eyes and a flatline mouth. When Roz didn't move fast or far enough to suit him, he knocked her halfway across the room with a deceptively casual backhand and then laughed when Sadie menaced him with a threat display.Runt though she was among drakena, she was roughly the same size as a drake---big enough to put up a fight.

The drake hissed at her and said,"You try anything and I'll kill both of these humans and make you watch while I eat them." When Sadie stood fast, hackles up and teeth bared, he ducked past her, prize-fighter quick, and punched Aurora in the mouth. "Make sure she gets the message," he told her as she crumpled to the ground. "I don't have to kill you quick."

"Mom!" Roz cried, and started toward her. At the same time, Sadie reared back to strike at the drake. Aurora stayed them both with an urgent upraised hand. For while the drakena might not have gotten the message, Aurora had: this mandrake would not have to work hard to dispatch any of them. Even Sadie, feisty as she was, was no match for his strength and savagery.. Surviving this predicament was going to be some seriously tricky business.

"Now is a time for thinking, not acting," she told the youngling. *"Be calm. Be ready. Do not let him provoke you into reacting."*

There were two mandrakes in the room now. The second one was smaller and darker -skinned than Drogo Channing and dressed like a desert prince. Bits of gore flecked the underside of his chin. Aurora got the distinct impression that the flesh and blood did not belong to him.

"Is this the runaway?" he asked, staring at Sadie as he sniffed at the air. "I thought she'd be bigger. Her smell isn't what I expected, either."

"Get away from her," Drogo snapped, and then shifted to block him from Sadie's sight. A moment later, the ambient smells of cooling tomato sauce and pepperoni gave way to a seriously funky musk. When Sadie stared at him, doing her best to project indifference, he curled his upper lip and struck a forceful pose. The funk grew more intense. Sadie remained steadfast. He flushed an unflattering shade of red and leveled a blazing glare at Roz.

"What's wrong with this drakena?" he snarled.

"Don't ask me," Roz replied, with a sullenness that may or may not have been feigned. "I barely know her."

The next thing Aurora knew, she was being hauled back onto her feet by her shirt front. Drogo sniffed her up and down like a spoiled side of beef and then hoisted her into his airspace. His breath reeked of carrion. She swallowed hard, partly to calm herself and partly to stifle her rising gorge. No one needed to tell her that there was no upside to barfing on a drake.

"You tell me then," he said. "What's wrong with the runaway?"

Aurora figured out what was bothering the mandrake almost immediately. Sadie wasn't responding to his pheromone-laden musk! But while her cognitive abilities had bounced back from that sucker-punch, her other faculties were still a little off. So, when some juvenile inner voice gloated about him having the draconic version of blue balls, her self-control slipped and she let out the tiniest of titters.

Drogo shook her like a rag doll and then blasted her with carrion-breath again. "You find humor in this situation? Do you understand how near to death you are?"

She nodded breathlessly even as she urged Sadie to hold steady.

"Sorry," she dared to say. "I tend to laugh when I'm nervous."

The mandrake narrowed his eyes as if he were trying to see all the way through to her core. Then he rubbed cheeks with her, marking her with his scent, and said, "What's wrong with the drakena? Why are you here? How many more of you are there?"

"Which question would you like me to answer first?" she asked, trying to sound contrite rather than contrary.

"I don't give a shit which reply you make first," he said. "Just tell me everything you know. Speak truthfully. I'll know if you're lying."

Liar. But he wasn't the only one who knew how to make stories up on the fly. And she had a doozy for him. It might amount to name-dropping. It might be the equivalent of throwing someone under a bus. Either way worked for her.

"Very well," she said. "This isn't all of us. One drakena is waiting for us in Mexico—"

"No, that is not right," Sadie interjected. *"Brigit went looking for water. She is likely nearby."*

Aurora ignored her. Time enough later to teach her about lies. Hopefully. Before she could build on her lie, though, Drogo interjected. "What about the third drakena? I heard there were three making this pilgrimage."

The fact that he had that kind of information unnerved Aurora for a moment. How much did he know? How did he know it? Fortunately, the truth fed right into her narrative. "She had a falling-out with the last of our group and abandoned us."

The mandrake scowled, clearly unhappy with the news, and gave her a menacing shake. "Who drove her off? You?"

She snorted, an as-if as daring as it was genuine. "One of your kind did it. His name is Grishka. Do you know of him?"

A look of pure hatred sizzled across the hardened contours of his face. Instinct urged her to recoil, but his hold on her had tightened reflexively. "Grishka," he said, sneering the name like the worst of insults. "He has much to answer for. Tezcatlipoca is furious with him."

"He knows," Aurora said. "He seeks to assuage the Great One's anger by presenting him with the two drakena. He means to surprise him."

Drogo sneered again. "A surprise? How inane! He becomes more and more human-like with every passing day. Where is he?"

"I don't know," she said, more truthful window-dressing. "He told us to come here and wait for him. We are here. We are waiting."

"Azi," he said, barking at his companion over his shoulder, "check the train schedules. That freak won't travel overland any other way." Then he turned his stainless-steel gaze back to Aurora. "You are bonded with this drakena, are you not?" he asked. At her nod, he went on to wonder, "Why would you assist Rasputin in returning her to Tezcatlipoca? You do know that he intends to turn her into breeding stock, don't you?"

She nodded and then scowled, a jaded grimace. "As you noted, she's a little unusual—"

"And how would you know that, human?" he asked.

There it was, the question that she'd been dreading and could not dodge. "I know because she's not the first drakena I've bonded with."

His eyes flattened only to go wide as he jumped to the inevitable conclusion. He laughed, a short, sharp, ugly bark, and said, "You're the woman Carlito was supposed to kill! You were bonded with Quetzalcoatl!" She tried not to flinch at the sound of her name, but apparently, her facial muscles betrayed her for the mandrake laughed again in diabolical delight. "I've never enjoyed killing anything so much. As old as she was, her blood tasted like lightning!"

Hate rang through Aurora's head, claxons and cacophonies and church bells all calling for apocalyptic action. She squeezed her eyes shut, blinking back furious tears, refusing to give the evil skink the satisfaction. He didn't even notice. Azi had finally gotten back to him with train schedules.

"There's nothing inbound until tomorrow afternoon."

"Excellent," Drogo said. "That gives us plenty of time to get ready for our ambush."

"Will we be setting up here or on the other side of the border?"

"He is coming here," Drogo said, "so we will take him here. While we are waiting for him, we should fortify ourselves. Subduing a full-grown drakena will take all of our strength."

Azi blinked, a slow lizard-like attempt to process a thought. "But—what about these three, Great One? Surely they will run away if we leave to go hunting."

"An astute observation, Azi," Drogo said, although it was clear by his tone that he had little respect for the other drake's intellect. "That is why I will hunt first. When I return, you will go and I will keep watch."

"We don't need to watch all of them, do we?" Azi asked, licking his lower lip as he eyed Roz. "That one's extra. We could just eat her."

"Jesus," Aurora heard Roz whisper, and she was thinking pretty much the same thing. Was it time to sic Sadie on them? The little drakena was ready and more than willing; Aurora could feel her struggling to keep herself focused and still. But how could Aurora pull that trigger, knowing that these drakes might then tear Sadie to shreds? How could she not, knowing that Roz would be killed if she didn't? As she agonized over a decision, Drogo gave her a relatively mild shake.

"We need this one to control the drakena," he said. "And we need that one," he went on, pointing at Roz, "to control this one." When Azi continued to balk, Drogo gave him an avuncular pat on the cheek. "Control is the essence of success. Azi. You would do well to remember that."

Azi made a grumpy hissing sound but argued no more. Drogo nodded approvingly and then added, "While I am gone, ward this room. No one else needs to know what's going on in here."

"Of course, Great One. It will be done."

Drogo nodded again and then unceremoniously slung Aurora aside. She staggered back several steps, lost her footing, and ended up butt-down on the floor. Sadie's temper flared at that, but Aurora managed to stop her from acting on the ensuing murderous impulse. She thought she had done so discreetly, but Drogo nodded directly at her afterward and said, "Good. Very good. Make sure you keep her in line while I am gone. When I return, we're going to talk more about her and her peculiarities. Who knows? If I like what I hear, I might even let you live."

Yeah, right. That sounded about as plausible as life on Pluto. But she'd worry about her own survival later. Right now, she needed to focus on saving the rest of their party. And since Azi had confiscated her cell phone, she had only one possible way of reaching out. It was a slim possibility at best, but she was desperate enough to try anything.

"*Your self-control was magnificent,*" she told Sadie, who had collapsed into a weary coil as soon as Drogo departed. "*Now close your eyes.*"

The pushback was immediate. "*This one does not want to sleep!*"

"*I don't want you to sleep,*" Aurora said. "*I want you to Dream.*"

CHAPTER 26

Grishka knew El Paso was going to be hot. He could feel the day's heat creeping into his sleeper car cubicle through the window, counteracting the air conditioning. Even so, he was not prepared for the hellish blast that slammed into him as he stepped onto the train station platform. It invaded his robes, his hair, his sinuses—a repulsive feeling. Although he had long since grown intolerant of the glacial winters that he had loved in his youth, he still preferred cooler to hotter, especially this so-called dry heat. Breathing air with no water in it was a chore.

He shuffled into the terminal and wandered from one end to the other, half-expecting to be accosted now that he was in Tezcatlipoca's territory. But while that Really Good someone was still stalking Grishka, he seemed content to do so from the shadows That changed things, Grishka thought, fingering the tangles of his beard. Possibly by a lot. Best not to speculate on such things, though. Speculation led to expectations which led to surprises and typically not the good kind.

He sought out an active air-conditioning vent and parked himself under it. As his sweat-slicked hide prickled with appreciation, he found his cell phone and tapped a pre-programmed number. Four rings later, a woman—possibly older, definitely Hispanic—answered. "Rio Bravo Motel. How can I help you?"

"I wonder if you could tell me if my friends have checked in yet," he said, projecting a bit of dragon charm. "They're in Room 119."

A pause ensued, and then: "Yes, they're here. Two men and two women."

The question popped out of him before he could catch it. "Two men?"

"Si. Big fellows. I saw them as I was getting ice." She paused for a microsecond and then added, "You sound surprised. Is everything OK? We don't want any trouble here."

"No need to worry," he said, pulsing another dose of 3G charm at her. "all is well. I just wasn't expecting them to be here so soon."

She tsked sympathetically. "You can't count on anyone to do what they say they're going to do anymore. Would you like me to connect you with the room?"

In the process of trying to both collect and reorder his thoughts, he didn't catch the offer at first and then hastened to refuse it. "Please don't," he said. "I want to return the favor and give them a little surprise. Could you tell me where exactly the room is?"

"First floor, south face. Room 119 is the casita at the far end of the row. You'll know it by the oversized patio. Is there anything else I can do for you?"

"Nothing at all," he replied. "Have a blessed evening." Then, as he eased the cellphone back into his knapsack, he said, "Rio Bravo Motel. First floor. South face. Last room in the row," like an old man committing directions to memory.

Then he started on his way, sure of his course if not its outcome.

Naga was in a foul mood. She hated being so far away from her territory. She hated the lack of options and decorum that came with eating on the fly. Most of all, she hated the heat. It came from all directions but especially the ground: wave after wave of ash-dry air that assaulted every sense.

"I can't believe anyone, man or drake, would choose to live in such a desolate part of the world," she grumbled to Lee, as they stalked the drake called Grishka. "This is demon country."

"You assume everyone has a choice in the matter," Lee replied flatly. "I assure you, such is not the case."

Naga chose to ignore the remark in favor of further griping. "If not for this facility's entirely inadequate air-conditioning, I would be suffocating already. My mouth and lungs are desiccated."

Lee heaved a long-suffering sigh. "Naga, you breath fire. I feel sure that you will survive a dose of low humidity." Then she went perfectly still, a sleek black-maned cat freezing at the sight of prey. *"Up ahead on the right? See?"*

Naga did not, but she trusted Lee's abilities and so froze as well. *"What's he doing?"*

"Sitting down." A moment later, she added, *"He's got his phone out."*

"Go and listen," Naga said, and just like that, Lee was gone even though it could mean her death if she got caught. Not that the odds of that happening were very high. Lee had a way of making herself unseen even when she was standing right in front of a body. And if by some fiendish turn of fate Grishka did sniff

her out, Naga would make sure that she came to no harm. Naga was much bigger than the drake. Naga was much stronger. The only thing about him that she had to fear was his musk.

For possibly the millionth time, she cursed the necessity of having to follow Grishka. But what else was she supposed to do? Somehow, he had convinced Brigit and Sadie that he was not a threat; not treacherous; not Tezcatlipoca's thrall. Worse, he had persuaded them to use him as a guide to the Great One's lair! Insanity! Naga had had the good sense to withdraw before Grishka could bespell her with his lies. That left her free to watch over her less sensible companions. And the best way to do that was to shadow the drake. Sooner or later, his actions would reveal his true intentions.

An impression brushed up against the thought like a cat seeking affection. It was faceless yet familiar, a vaguely unsavory sense of déjà vu. As Naga struggled to put a name to what she was feeling, the sense nudged her again, broadcasting urgent mixed messages.

Hurry!

Beware!

Help!

Then—nothing.

Naga was not the avid traveler of the Dreaming that Quetzalcoatl had been, but she was no stranger to its tug. Not once, however, had it tried to engage her while she was fully awake. Leastwise, not until now. She did not know who the interloping Dreamer was, but she had her suspicions.

Aurora Vanderbilt.

Who else could it be?

Quetzalcoatl had been her mentor. Their bond had the Dreaming woven all through it. And Naga had caught a fleeting glimpse of the Great One during the contact. Naga gnashed her teeth, mincing her resentment into gall-stained pieces. That woman had the most perverse sort of luck! At times it allowed her to do remarkable, never-done things. Other times, it was like an oil spill, tainting everything in its path. Given the circumstances, Naga had to believe that this was an Exxon Valdez kind of day.

Lee was standing at Naga's elbow now, exercising a form of discipline that only looked like patience. At some other time or place, Naga might have toyed with her for a while, testing her restraint. Today, however, she had too many things on her mind.

"What did he say?" she asked.

"Rio Bravo Motel. First floor. South face. Last room in the row."

"That must be where Brigit and the others are," Naga surmised, and then fell silent as she tried to piece what little information she had into their next move. The only plan she came up with was distressingly uninspired. "We will go there, too, and keep watch."

That provoked a throat-noise from Lee that could be construed as either scandalized or reproachful. "You mean to spy on our own?"

"Yes."

"Why?" Lee asked.

"Because I do not trust Aurora," Naga said. "Pure coincidence cannot account for all the trouble she attracts. It could be that she and Rasputin have made other, secret arrangements that favor drakes rather than drakena."

"What are you talking about?" Lee said, with a scowl that matched the throat-sound.

"Brigit is more of a prize to the drakes than Saidhe is," Naga said. "It may be that Aurora means to give her to the drakes in Saidhe's stead. It may be that she means to expose me to them, too."

There was no mistaking the sound Lee made next for anything other than shock. "Do you really think Aurora would do that to her own daughter's dragon?"

Naga reached out and tipped Lee's chin up until their gazes met. "What would you do to protect your dragon?" Lee tried to say something, but Naga would not let her. "You would do anything. I know you would. So would Aurora. Therefore, we must be braced for treachery. It may be that Quetzalcoatl tried to warn me of that possibility."

Lee shifted, ending their rapport but Naga could still sense the conflict in her, that feeling of loyalties being stretched. Naga did not understand Lee's quandary. She had never held Aurora in particularly high regard. If anything, Naga would have expected her to have more empathy for Roz-a-lyn.

"Why do you defend her?" Naga wondered aloud.

"Because she has been twice-Chosen," Lee replied. "That was The Divine's doing. If you believe in The Divine, then you must believe in Aurora, too."

Naga could not fault Lee's logic, but neither could she embrace it. There was something off about Aurora Vanderbilt. She just couldn't put a dew claw on it—yet.

But the day was still young.

CHAPTER 28

"Wake up."

The command came with a glancing blow to the head. Aurora tried to rouse herself, but the Dreaming held firm. A second, more emphatic blow ensued. It snapped her halfway back to consciousness. "I said—wake up!"

Aurora raised an arm over her head, an instinctive attempt to ward off a third cuff. As she did so, Sadie pulsed her a groggy thought. *Time to rise?* Aurora urged her back to sleep, knowing even half-awake that the youngling was safer in her dreams for the nonce.

"Okay, okay," she grumbled then, shifting onto the bones of her butt. "I'm up. What do you want?"

Drogo was staring down at her, radiating the kind of hunger that can't ever be satisfied. His lips had a pinkish tinge. His cheeks were downright rosy. He reeked of sweat and fresh gore. "I have questions. You have answers. Speak them."

"What do you want to know?" she asked, playing for time because that was the only play she had. "Mind if I get some water? The air conditioning has dried me right out."

"You stay," he said, pointing at her like a dog. Then he turned that imperious finger on Roz and said, "You get the water. And open the back door while you're at it. This place reeks of pizza." This even though the pizza was long gone, eaten by Azi straight off the tiles an instant after Drogo had left to go hunting. "Now," he said to Aurora, while pointing at Sadie, "tell me more about that one. Why does she not respond to me? Has Grishka Rasputin altered her in some way? Has he—?" He paused, struck by a thought that raised his color along with his brow ridges. "Has he managed to impregnate her already?" A look like wonder ghosted across his face only to vanish as he laughed. "Ha! Tezcatlipoca gets his breeder back but cannot breed with her! What a delicious trick! I'm almost tempted to let that freak go through with his plan just to witness The Great One's fury when he learns that his hope for the next age is carrying the cripple's spawn."

By then, Roz was back with a plastic cup of water. As she handed it over to Aurora, she made a discreet what-now face. Any number of responses occurred to Aurora. 'Call Brigit' was one—but she supposed her daughter had already tried that. 'Stay on your toes' was another. As if anyone could relax in such an adrenaline-infused atmosphere. 'Don't do anything stupid' was a third, but that ship had sailed when they decided to go forward with this misadventure. Naga had been right to call it quits.

I will not come to your aid.

Drogo batted Roz back into her corner and then resumed his gloating. "I do not know which gives me more pleasure: the thought of killing Rasputin or the thought of thwarting his plans."

Even though Aurora knew that Naga had turned her back on them and was too far away to help, she had still tried to contact her through the Dreaming. But riding that slipstream with a barely grown drakena was a vastly different experience than riding it with one as experienced as Quetzalcoatl. She'd had no control, no control at all. The Dreaming carried them where it would, zinging from past to future to past like a hummingbird on speed. At one point, she thought she had made contact with the ill-humored Loong. A moment later, though, she was being whisked away to a brilliant green jungle by a pink-frilled behemoth. She understood none of it. Nothing at all. Then Drogo had slapped her awake.

"I confess, I am eager to see his ridiculous face," the mandrake was saying now. "Call him. Tell him you are here and waiting for him."

"I would," she said, "but your minion confiscated our cell phones and dumped them in the toilet."

Drogo heaved a sigh of phony dismay. "Ah, Azi. He means well, but lacks the ability to think things through before he acts. No matter, though. Rasputin will be here soon enough. When he arrives, I mean to tear out his throat."

The front door swung open with a casual creak. Azi returning, Aurora supposed, but in shambled Grishka instead. He looked even more disheveled than usual. Oddly enough, that made him seem more dignified than laughable.

"Is that all you can talk about?" he asked, as he hobbled into the room. "Throat-tearing? What a dull-witted drake you are, Drogo Channing."

Drogo cast Aurora aside like a forgotten rag doll. She landed on her butt next to Roz, who was quick to pull her into a semi-protective, semi-comforting embrace. Meanwhile, still smiling, Drogo squared off in front of Grishka.

"Surprised to see me?" he asked, all but purring.

"Not really," Grishka replied, fingering the tangles of his beard like he always did when he wanted to put Drogo on edge. "The Divine sees all. Sometimes She reveals all, too."

"Did She show you your death?" Drogo crooned. "Was it wearing my face?"

"Death is better-looking than you," Grishka said. "But if you wish to test my mettle, step forth. I have been tested by better than the likes of you."

"We shall see," Drogo said, hissing the last word as he transitioned back into a drake. And what a drake he became: richly muscled and robust, with powerful arms and jaws.

Grishka seemed almost sickly by comparison: less vital and less vicious, more like a road-weary daddy drake who would have rather been heading for the bottom of a pond. Nevertheless, he squared off against Drogo and began to sway—a slow, surprisingly seductive forth-and-back, forth-and-back. Aurora could feel the power of the spell he was trying to cast, but if it had any impact on Drogo, the drake showed no sign of it. He watched the dance for a moment, a mix of contempt and excitement burning in his gold eyes. Although Aurora could not hear the conversation in her head, she had no doubt that he was heaping insults on Grishka.

As if in response to such provocation, Grishka reared back and spat—not a stream of dragon fire but rather a large, tar-like glob that splashed and then sizzled as it struck the top of Drogo's shoulder. Drogo snarled, a pained sound that arched into fury. Grishka loosed another gout. Drogo could have dodged the salvo, but chose instead to take it full in the chest as if to demonstrate how little he thought of Grishka's venom. And before Grishka could strike again, Drogo attacked. One instant he was scornfully disengaged; the next, his jaws were clamped around Grishka's throat. Aurora sucked in a breath, preparing herself for a geyser of dragon blood. Drogo, however, was in no rush to deliver the coup de gras. Instead, he chose to torment Grishka, pressing down but not quite biting through his neck. Grishka's only options were to endure the torture or provoke a bite reflex. Thus far, he was staying very still.

"Shit!" Roz whispered, an audible cringe. In an even lower tone, she added, "Let's get out of here!"

The suggestion snapped Aurora out of her fascinated daze. Of course! This was their chance! She reached out with a thought, meaning to rouse Sadie. As she did so, Azi strolled into the room through the back patio. The mandrake licked his thin lips as he made eye contact with Aurora and then lit up like a downtown Christmas tree when he looked past her.

"Ah, excellent!" he said, his accent waxing sibilant. "I am in time for the finale!." He tapped Roz on the knee with an overlong fingernail and winked. "Watch carefully. This is what I am going to do—to you."

Those last two words lit Aurora up like a jolt of lightning. She had to get Roz the hell out of here—at any cost! And Sadie was going to have to help! "Wake up now!" she urged, as Drogo continued his domination of Grishka. *"Wake up and fly away with Roz!"*

CHAPTER 29

Naga and Lee were hunkered down on a rooftop that overlooked the back end of the Rio Bravo Motel. The sun was sinking. The temperature, however, remained sweltering. The spiced, deep-fried exhaust from the restaurant across the street clung to the overheated air like a greasy perfume. The smells made Naga hungry.

"You should go over there and get me something to eat," she said to Lee, infusing the thought with psychic drool.

"When we are done watching," Lee replied from her hiding place, and then went on to add, *"When will that be?"*

"When we have seen enough," Naga said, a retort meant to shut down the conversation. But Lee had her own agenda.

"When will enough be enough?" she asked. *"Will you cling to your mistrust of Aurora Vanderbilt forever?"*

Naga's nostrils flared red, a display of affront. *"Cautiousness is a virtue. You would do well to cultivate more of it."*

"You seek to distract me, but I will not be diverted," Lee said, projecting adamancy even as she focused on the motel room across the way. *"Tell me truly. Do you have it in you to forgive that woman for being unlucky?"*

"Does she truly seem unlucky to you?" Naga countered. *"A dominant drake invaded her warded safe-place and yet she still lives. An unlucky person would be dead by now. An unlucky person would have watched her daughter and maybe her drakena die first. My guess is that the two of them are allies and that they're waiting for their fellow conspirator, the drake named Rasputin, to arrive."*

"And then what?" Lee asked, more of a challenge than a query.

"I do not know," Naga replied. *"That is why we are here, watching. I can tell you this much, however. If Aurora is conspiring with those drakes, I will see that she draws her last breath tonight."*

Lee's thoughts tightened like a fist, but before she could throw another punch in Aurora's defense, Naga shut the discussion down with a hiss. *"Rasputin has entered the safe place!"* she announced, twitching her tail in what could have either been excitement or annoyance. *"Saidhe says he seems quite sure of himself."* A moment later, Naga's tail twitched again. *"The little one is upset—no, she is angry! Angry because Drogo Channing just tossed Aurora across the room. She wants to attack the mandrake, but Aurora is preventing her. I wonder why."*

"She's protecting the youngling," Lee said.

"That's one theory, I suppose," Naga said, although she was more focused on the relay from Saidhe than her link with Lee.

A roar echoed out of the room and into the gathering gloam. A second, less vociferous roar followed. Neither one of them needed Saidhe to tell them that a challenge had been issued—and accepted. *"The youngling says they are Changing!"* Naga said, relaying echoes of Saidhe's awe and excitement as well. *"Drogo Channing is very well made! Djadja looks a bit—broken."* A suspenseful pause ensued and then: *"Drogo is insulting Djadja's inferior lineage and looks, but Djadja will not be provoked. Instead of charging Drogo, he begins to—dance? He sways forth and back, forth and back, moving with a suppleness than the youngling has never seen—"*

"Naga, someone else is heading toward that room."

"Describe the newcomer!" Naga said, straining to maintain her own train of thought as well as two others.

"Human-sized, maybe a little larger—"

Saidhe hissed—a sound both shocked and excited. *"Drogo Channing has seized Djadja by the throat!"*

"Looks like a man, moves like a drake," Lee went on, oblivious to the opposing narrative. "My guess is mandrake. I do not recognize him."

A wave of surprise crashed through Naga, then childish curiosity. "*Why does Drogo not bite down? He is clearly the dominant—Wait! Aurora is urging this one to get up now. She says she is going to create a diversion so this one and Roz can escape. What does that mean? What is 'diversion'?*"

Just like that, all of Naga's suspicions avalanched, exposing a glaring new reality. An instant later, Naga was on her feet and gliding over the lip of the rooftop.

"*Wait!*" Lee called after her. "*What are you doing?*"

"*Something I never thought I would do,*" she replied, as she sailed toward the ground. "*I'm going to save that wretched woman's life.*"

CHAPTER 30

"Dammit, Brigit! Where the hell are you?" Roz said, a psychic shout that bristled with urgency. *"As soon as Drogo is finished toying with Grishka, he's going to start in on us! And,"* she added, as Azi leered at her like lunchmeat, *"his sidekick might not wait that—"*

Long, she was about to say, but even as the word took shape in her head, Aurora grabbed her hand and slung her toward the bathroom. She motioned for Saidhe to go that way, too. "Lock the door behind you," she said, under her breath, "then climb out the window."

"Nuh-uh," Roz said, braking hard. "Not without you."

Her mother sputtered, the sound of homogenized fear and frustration. "Just do it!" she snapped, and then shifted to put herself between Roz and Azi. The mandrake grinned, baring a tidy set of serrated teeth. "You challenge me to protect your offspring," he said, closing in on her step by casual step. "I like that. It whets the appetite. When I am done with you, she will taste all the sweeter."

"Bring it, meathead," Aurora said. An instant later, she cast a wide-eyed scowl at Sadie. It was a look that Roz remembered from her youth, a look that said, 'Do as I say right now!'

Instead, Saidhe launched herself at Azi.

Aurora shouted, "No!"

Grishka let out a strangled half-croak, half-roar.

Then the patio door exploded, spraying glass everywhere. An instant later, a magnificent golden dragon charged into the room, hissing and spitting like fury itself. Drogo pivoted toward the commotion, slinging Grishka aside in the process. By then, Naga had already bitten Azi's head off. His decapitated body flopped and flailed on the floor for a moment, coating the debris field of shattered glass with sizzling ichor. A moment later, the corpse turned to ash. Meanwhile, Roz grabbed Aurora's arm and tried to drag her toward the hole in the back wall. Aurora took a few dazed steps but then abruptly dug in her heels.

"Sadie!" she called, shouting to make herself heard over the riot of snapping and snarling that was going on. "Let's go now! Hurry!"

Sadie ignored her, choosing instead to stand side by side with Naga. The great Loong did not appear to notice Sadie's presence. Her gaze was focused on Drogo. Likewise, his attention was all for Naga. As he stared at her, he reared up, rampant, and a familiar musk crept back into the room. Naga's nostrils flared. Her breathing took on a strained note.

"He is admiring her size and robustness," Lee said, appearing at Roz's elbow. "He says he is going to—" She flinched as if stung and then flushed, mirroring Naga's reactions. "He has promised to do unspeakable things to her."

In response to that bit of dragon pillow talk, Naga reared up: both a rejection and a threat. The muscles in her midsection flexed. Her jaws were clenched. Yet she made no move to attack. Roz elbowed Lee: an unsubtle prompt to prod her dragon back to the here-and-now. But Lee was locked in the same kind of stasis. Her cheeks were flushed; her breathing, ragged.

"What in hell is going on?" she whispered.

Lee glanced up at Roz, the briefest of glimpses, as if she were afraid that she would lose her composure if she broke focus for too long.

"Naga is responding," she whispered. "Drogo's musk is powerful."

All at once, Roz understood what was going on. Shit! How could she not after that time in the train station? On that occasion, Bridge's object of desire had been a man and the psychic spill-over had damn near sent Roz slavering after the barman. That had been a cerebral affair compared to the hormonal firestorm that was taking place here. Roz couldn't even imagine what Lee was feeling right now.

"Run!" Roz said. "You should get as far away from here as you can."

"No," Lee said, grinding the refusal out through gritted teeth. "My place is here—with—Naga. She needs my—strength. You and your mother are the ones who should go. Naga wishes it."

The rims of Naga's nostrils were white with strain. Her tongue flicked back and forth from a gap in her teeth, but this was not a threat display. It was desperation. It was disbelief. It was— desire. As the drakena struggled to hold her ground against Drogo's fetid allure, Lee let out a whimper and grabbed Roz's arm with dragon-like strength. Roz could not help but marvel at the potency of draconic pheromones. It had brought a full-grown, strong-willed drakena to a standstill and possibly to her knees. How terrible to be held prisoner by one's own biology.

Naga let out a rumble under her breath, broadcasting resistance even as it failed within. The drake rumbled in turn, a sound of hunger and triumph. He closed in on her, his intentions obviously carnal. With a screech, Sadie flung herself at him. Drogo ended her charge with a casual-seemingly swat that slammed her into the far wall. She rebounded like a dragon-shaped ball and then staggered for her footing. As she did so, Drogo snarled at her.

"He says he will kill you if this one persists," Sadie told Aurora. *"He says he will kill all of us if this one interferes again."*

"Great," Aurora muttered.

Roz jumped on the utterance in a heartbeat.

"What?" she whispered.

Aurora sighed. "Nothing good."

"What should this one do?" Sadie asked then. *"Naga wants this one to flee—but not really. Deep down, Naga wants this one to save her along with you and the others. This one thinks it would be easier to flee. But this one does not want to leave. Naga belongs to us."*

"Yes," Aurora echoed, speaking aloud for Roz's benefit. "Naga belongs with us. And it doesn't feel right to run. But to tell you the truth, I don't think we can bust her out of this mess."

A rumble that sounded vaguely like, "I can," rose up from the vicinity of the front door. Drogo ignored the sound, preferring to gloat over spellbound Naga. Roz and the others turned that way to see Grishka shake off the last of his daze and climb back onto his feet. He raised a gnarled claw to his muzzle, a draconic, 'Shhh!' A moment later, he threw himself onto Drogo's back. Drogo roared, projecting more irritation than surprise, and then tried to shake off the other drake. Grishka held tight. Drogo tried again and again, throwing himself backward into one wall and then another. The wall sprouted a drake-sized dents, but Grishka hung on like a bronco buster.

"Shit," Roz said, an awed whisper. "Check that out. I didn't think the old guy had it in him."

"Yeah, well, the round's not over yet," Aurora said, and then tugged on her daughter's arm. "C'mon. Let's jet while the jetting is good."

But there was no escape, not really, not with Drogo thrashing about in his ever-wilder attempts to dislodge Grishka. *"Drogo is angry with Djadja,"* Sadie relayed to Aurora. *"He says Djadja does not fight like a dragon. This one does not understand what that means. Djadja is a dragon. How could he not fight like one?"*

Aurora sneered. *"Don't listen to Drogo. He's just trying to*

provoke Grishka."
"Into what?"
"Into getting off his back, I guess."
"Curious."

Just then, Drogo let out a frustrated roar and craned his head, straining to sink his teeth into whatever part of Grishka that he could reach. In doing so, he exposed his throat. Quick as a thought, Grishka thrust a jagged claw into the underside of Drogo's jaw and dragged it across his throat. A chasm opened up in slow motion. A moment later, blood began oozing from the wound like lava. Drogo made a gurgling sound—surprise perhaps or possibly disbelief. Then he glanced at Naga, who was still befuddled by his scent, and disbelief dissolved into regret. Roz did not need to hear his thoughts to know what he was thinking: Close! So close! He'd nearly had everything his way!

"Almost but not quite," Roz murmured aloud.

His gaze flicked her way, an act of sheer will and contempt. As he peered at her, he quite deliberately defecated—and then slumped lifeless to the ground.

For one interminable moment afterward, nobody moved. The only thing Roz could do was gape at that huge pile of shit on the floor and think, dear God, that could've been someone she knew. Then Naga shuddered and snorted like someone rousing from a bad dream. Her return to the here-and-now released everyone else from their stasis. Aurora went to check on Sadie. Lee reunited with Naga. Naga consulted with her Chosen for a moment and then headed out the back way alone.

"Where's she going?" Roz asked, all jittery and jumpy from excess adrenaline. "Is she coming back?"

"Naga needs to clear her head," Lee replied. "This incident was somewhat stressful for her."

Roz felt a wisecrack bubbling forth from her hypoglycemic

brain, something to the effect of join-the-club. Before she could eke it out, though, Lee went on. "Naga also says that the wards that were cast over this room are crumbling. We will need to move on—soon."

"Roger that," Roz said. "We'll jet just as soon as Bridge gets back."

Just then, Brigit came strolling into the room, glancing this way like a tourist on a walking tour. *"A canna say tha A like what ye've done with tha place,"* she remarked. *"Tha innkeepers are going ta be pissed."*

"Yeah, well," Roz said, relaxing in places that she hadn't known were tense, "they can keep the deposit. And oh, by the way—where the fuck have you been? We could have been killed."

"A was at tha bottom of the river when ye called," Brigit replied, utterly unapologetic. *"A came as quickly as A could, but there were lots of people ta dodge."* She froze then, and began sniffing the air excitedly. *"What is that incredible smell?!?"*

Roz pointed at the heap of dragon shit on the floor. "Drogo's eloquent fare-the-well."

But Brigit wasn't looking at Drogo's droppings. Her attention was fixed on Grishka.

CHAPTER 31

Aurora rented a beat-up box truck that reeked of stale cigarette smoke and human sweat. Roz drove it into the mountains; Grishka rode shotgun to show her the way. Everyone else hung out in the trailer. Brigit slept; Lee and Naga communed. Aurora sat with her back against a grimy wheel well and Sadie-Dragon's head in her lap. The drakena was churring contentedly, a sound that coaxed Aurora's cortisol levels back toward normal levels. Despite the utter lack of creature comforts and the ambient stink (to which she was no doubt contributing), she felt oddly content, at peace with where they were heading and what they planned to do. Maybe the feeling stemmed from battle-fatigue. Maybe it came from a cell-deep desire to be done with this epic, life-altering adventure. Whatever the cause, though, Aurora was not alone in feeling it. The entire troupe was in synch now, even Naga, who prided herself in always going her own way. Her experience with Drago Channing had left her shaken and borderline humbled. Aurora mostly felt sorry for her for having been so sorely tested. But one tiny vindictive inner voice was grimly pleased that she had been brought down a peg. No hurt, no foul, and maybe somebody had learned something, right?

The truck rocked like a wagon-train, back and forth, mile after mile, and eventually lulled Aurora to sleep. As soon as she nodded off, the Dreaming came for her—almost as if it had been lying in wait. Together with Sadie, she went spiraling through time and space. She saw her house as it was when it was first built. She caught a glimpse of Duncan, too, but was swept away before she could do anything but blow a heart-kiss his way. Charles appeared, his ugliness exposed, and then a great black drake; together, they spilled oceans of human blood. Horror reared in Aurora, and searing disbelief. How had she not seen what a monster her ex-lover was? And his master was worse—evil made flesh! Ending him was going to be a pleasure! Sadie echoed the thought with a psychic chirp and then chirped again as a pink-frilled dragon emerged from the carnage. The drakena tried to nose Aurora into another slipstream, but Aurora resisted. She wanted to take in every last fleck of gore so she would be in the proper mindset when it came time to kill Tezcatlipoca. Quetzalcoatl warbled her concern—

—and then abrupted disappeared as the truck shuddered to a rickety stop. Moments later, the cargo door scrolled open and Roz stuck her head in the trailer. "Damn!" she said, recoiling instantly. "You guys smell worse than a sheep-pen on a hot day." She put a hand over her mouth and nose, then added, "Get on out of there!"

They disembarked, two women and three drakena. Six months ago, Aurora would have been freaking out about such a fantastical grouping. Now she was more worried about her hygiene. Did she really smell like a sheep pen?

"I thought it would be harder than this," Roz said, as she and the others followed Grishka down a rough, stone-hewn path to Tezcatlipoca's lair. "I thought we'd have to fight our way in or something."

Grishka snorted. Brigit was quick to provide a translation which Roz then shared with Aurora. "He says this place does not need to be guarded because it is warded, and that if he had not led us here, we never would have found it. Also, this mountain has an unsavory reputation so most humans avoid it. Those few who don't are either agents—or livestock."

The hair on the back of Aurora's neck prickled as if Charles had just run a ghostly hand across her nape. He would have been familiar with this place. He would have known that people were being butchered here. If what the Dreaming had shown her was real, then he had taken an active part in the slaughter. Her stomach churned—distress mixed with outrage. The bastard had gotten what he deserved! And yet—

And yet—

Shit! She was going to need therapy to work through this one.

They came to an intersection in the hollowed-out shaft that they were following. The drake nodded at the downward-sloping tunnel. Roz said, "Sadie's siblings are being housed in an underground grotto one level down. Grishka wants Sadie to go and release them. He wants you to go with her, Mom."

Resistance blazed through her, hot as dragon fire. No way she was going to consent to being sent to the rear, not after all she had suffered because of Tezcatlipoca! Sadie felt the same way for the same reason.

"You go, sweetie," she said. "Sadie and I have come for our pound of flesh, and we mean to have it."

"Mother!" Roz said, breaking the word into two distinct, unhappy halves. "You have to go! I can't leave Bridge!" And it was clear that Brigit wouldn't be parting company with Grishka anytime soon. Since his triumph over Drogo, the drakena's attraction to him had ballooned into near-obsession. Aurora knew that Roz wasn't particularly happy about the situation, but if there was one quality about her daughter that stood out above all else, it was her loyalty to family and friends. Even so, Aurora refused to concede.

"Then I guess we're just going to have to free the younglings later," she said. "They've waited this long. What's an hour more?"

"But—Mom," Roz said, in that urgent, childish way she

had when she wanted something really-really bad. "What if we don't—" She paused, trying to find a nice way to say 'fail'. "What if something goes wrong? All of this will have been for nothing."

The plea had no impact on Aurora's resolve. As she opened her mouth to say so, Lee called out from the rear-guard. "Naga and I will go." The offer provoked a volley of raised eyebrows. She dismissed the group's surprise with a shrug and added, "Naga does not care to expose herself to another drake at the moment."

Naga's admission of vulnerability made Aurora regret her earlier snarkiness. Naga had challenged Drogo even though she knew that doing so could cost her everything that she held dear. Who knew what would have happened if she had decided to sit the fight out instead? And who hadn't bitten off more than they could chew at one time or another?

"Does this meant that Naga is not the only one who has learned something?"

The thought caught Aurora off-guard. There was no emotion attached to it, no judgment, only the faintest hint of slyness that Sadie must have learned from Grishka. It was a sharp little reminder that the drakena, while still young, was not a child. She was a dragon, fair and square. Aurora offered her partner in crime a psychic cheek-rub and then said, "Let's be like Naga. Let's do this."

Roz didn't know if she was more excited or more afraid; the two felt the same, especially when there was a drakena humming in your head. It was a near-mindless broadcast: Brigit trying to displace her burgeoning horniness and declining self-control. She watched Grishka Rasputin's every move and followed slavishly on his heels as he lumbered from one gold-flecked tunnel to the next. It seemed that her only reason for breathing was to inhale more of his increasingly rank musk. Roz hung well back from the drakena to preserve her sanity. Aurora noticed her distancing herself and closed in to check on her.

"Are you OK?" she whispered.

"Why wouldn't I be?" Roz replied, a sarcastic quip. "I'm on my way to confront a former god with a drakena who's jonesing so hard for dragon sex that she can barely see straight. And if I get too close to her, my vision starts to blur, too."

Aurora responded with a look of grim sympathy. "Not exactly the kind of problem you encounter every day, is it?"

"No shit, Mom," Roz replied, realizing only after the fact that she was edgier than she'd imagined. "What in hell possessed us to come here? The potential for disaster is astronomically high."

"We're here in our own defense," Aurora said, surprisingly resolute. "And—because our dragons need us."

The tunnel they were following turned upward and to the left. As they rounded that bend, a dim light appeared. Roz had no doubt that it was a train. The vicious, fire-breathing kind. She reached for her mother's hand. At the same time, Aurora reached for hers. A moment later, Brigit relayed instructions from Grishka.

"He says tha meeting chamber is just ahead. He urges ewe and yer mum ta wait outside while we treat with Tezcatlipoca. He says tha Great One's only love fer humans is gustatory and he is nae a good sport."

Point taken.

Yet safer or not, hiding out in the wings did not sit well with Roz. She was used to being part of the vanguard if not a ringleader. So, when they finally reached the chamber, Roz waited until the dragons went on ahead and then snuck through the entryway for a better look. Moments later, Aurora joined her.

The chamber was a massive cavern that had the look and feel of an ancient amphitheater. It was lit by an array of shallow, floor-based firepits. The fires danced with looming shadows, a shimmery interplay. Roz hadn't been expecting beauty in such an ill-omened place, but beautiful it was in a stark, subterranean sort of way. She peeked over a ledge of rock that rimmed the basin and then watched as Grishka, flanked by Brigit and Sadie, hobbled down the rough-hewn slope. The drake seemed more cumbersome than usual, and less sure of his footing. Roz supposed his recent smack-down with Drogo was to blame for that. She just hoped that he still had something left in the tank for Tezcatlipoca. If Brigit had to handle that evil lizard by herself—

"Shut the feck up. A'm quite capable of doing what needs tae be done."

Oops. Wrong inner voice.

As the trio closed in on the center of the bowl, a large black drake with a jaguar's golden eyes strode onto the chamber's far lip. Even from this distance, Roz could see that the drake was far older than Grishka. His musculature was leathery; his stride, stilted. But—those eyes! Aged or not, they took in everything and gave nothing back. He rumbled, the first to break silence. She gave Brigit a psychic nudge, demanding a live feed. Brigit was not happy with the intrusion, but obliged nonetheless. In the wariest of whispers, Roz then shared with Aurora.

"Greetings, Grishka," Tezcatlipoca said. "I confess, I was extremely displeased when you ignored my calls and then sent a message telling me to expect your arrival. But now I see what it was that kept you away and then brought you back. Two drakena, one of them full-grown! What a prize!"

Grishka rumbled, the draconic equivalent of a modest throat-clearing. "Actually, I have three drakena with me—two of them full-grown."

Roz could almost feel amazement geyser from Tezcatlipoca like high-end champagne. "Three drakena? I confess, Grishka Rasputin, you have eclipsed all expectation! How did you manage to subdue them—and keep them subdued! Look! They offer no resistance at all! What strange power do you have over them?"

"No power at all, Great One," Grishka replied. "They are here of their own free will."

Tezcatlipoca smacked his lips, a display of pleasure and delight, then leered at Brigit. When she failed to respond, he dismissed her with a snort and said, "Where is the third one? Summon her now. I wish to behold her."

"Soon enough," Grishka promised, sounding wry rather than coy. "At the moment, she is freeing Saidhe's clutch-mates."

"Who?"

Saidhe warbled, a proud, "This one!"

If Tezcatlipoca heard her, he showed no sign of it. He was still trying to work through Grishka's tease. "Freeing?" he said, leaning into the word as if he had never heard it before. "Why would she—? What purpose—" He stopped, dumbstruck by a thought. The puzzlement that he had been projecting avalanched, revealing a contemptuous new facade "So," he said, "you and Drogo Channing have joined forces."

"Not so," Grishka said, projecting gravity with just a touch of slyness.

"Do your drakena know what Drogo intends to do to their precious world?" Tezcatlipoca snarled, and then turned his outraged disbelief on Brigit. "Did he tell you that Drogo wants to wipe out all of mankind? Why would you support such madness? We cannot be gods is there is no one to worship us."

"You fear the wrong things," Grishka said. "Drogo Channing and I are not allied. Drogo is dead. I know because I killed him."

The bluntness of the statement startled Tezcatlipoca, causing him to rear back a little. He did not recover immediately, either, which Roz found gratifying. Score one for Grish!

"I do not believe you," Tezcatlipoca said finally. "Drogo is—formidable. You—are not."

Grishka snorted ever so softly. "A river that twists and turns is a powerful thing still. So it is with me," he said. "And—I have been known to exaggerate my disabilities when doing so is to my advantage."

"It's not exaggerating when you do it all the time," Tezcatlipoca said. Then, with a blink of those cold, golden eyes, he shuttered his agitation and became inscrutable again. "Maybe you killed Drogo," he said. "Maybe you didn't. If you did, you saved me the trouble of having to end him. If you didn't, I will attend to him presently—after I attend to you."

"I don't think so," Grishka said, maintaining his neutral pose even as the great drake sank into a predatory crouch. "I believe it is I who will be attending to you."

Tezcatlipoca's short-fused outrage returned, igniting an explosion of activity. The Great One launched himself. Grishka shifted to dodge the charge. Then Brigit rushed in like a battering ram and knocked Tezcatlipoca to the ground. An instant later, she was tightly coiled around his midsection. He fought to free himself, but she was bigger than him, stronger and more flexible, too. She let him writhe for a moment, enjoying his struggles, but then closed her jaws over the soft side of his throat—just hard enough for him to feel the prick of her fish-hook teeth. Roz was stunned by the drakena's savage aplomb. She had never seemed so utterly daunting—and Roz had seen her tear a man into pieces!

Tezcatlipoca glared at Grishka, radiating a hate that filled the entire basin. "That's how it is then," he said. "You will kill me and then surrender the next age to the drakena, who will then hand it over to their apelings." He shifted his gaze in Brigit's direction. "Why?" he asked. "They destroy everything they touch."

"Not everything," Brigit replied flatly. "And ye enslaved yer own kind to serve yer own ambition. Go ahead an' tell me how tha makes ye better than them."

"He helped!" Tezcatlipoca said, trying to drag Grishka under the same bus that he now found himself. "It was his idea!"

"A know," Brigit said. "The difference is, he has regrets. Ewe—do not."

The great drake made a rude noise and then went limp, giving Brigit even more access to his throat than she had had already. "If you are going to kill me, then get on with it already," he said. "The name of my only regret is Rasputin."

Brigit and Grishka exchanged a look. A decision passed between them, too. But before either of them could act on it, Aurora popped to her feet and shouted, "Don't! Don't do it!"

All eyes turned her way. Tezcatlipoca growled under his breath and then snorted steam. "I should have known you would bring monkeys with you."

"She argues for your life, Great One,'" Grishka said, a surprisingly gentle chiding. "You might want to treat her with a modicum of respect." When Tezcatlipoca responded with a second puff of steam, Grishka made an un-dragon-like clucking sound and then turned his attention to Aurora. At that moment, Roz saw him not as bent or broken, but weathered like driftwood and weirdly beautiful.

Or maybe she was just seeing through Brigit's overstimulated eyes.

"Why would you spare him?" he asked through Sadie. "He has caused you and the little one more harm than anyone else here."

Aurora grimaced, an outward sign of an internal struggle. "Quetzalcoatl wishes him to live."

"How do you know?" he pressed. "The Great One is dead."

"She lives on in the Dreaming," Aurora said. "Sadie and I encountered her there on the trip here." Tezcatlipoca sneered. Brigit rewarded him with a nip close to his jugular. "I didn't understand what she was telling me at first," Aurora went on, "but I've had plenty of time to think about it. She doesn't want him killed. That would just be revenge."

"What's so wrong with that?" Roz blurted, springing out of her crouch. "He's murdered thousands. If we don't stop him, he'll murder thousands more."

"Perhaps," Aurora granted. "But our task wasn't to avenge his victims, was it. It was to stop him from claiming the next age. And—he has been stopped. His would-be stable has been freed. His closest allies are no longer available to him."

"Yes, but—" Roz started, remembering that TV image of her home ablaze.

"The killing has to stop somewhere, baby girl," Aurora said. "Why not here? We're not dragon-slayers."

A pause ensued, everyone waiting for Roz to counter. When she remained silent, Grishka rumbled approvingly. "For far too long now, men and dragons have killed each other mostly out of habit," he said. "It takes strength—and vision—to dare a new path." He returned his attention to Tezcatlipoca, whose sneer had wilted beneath the weight of uncertainty. "I am with Aurora," he said. "I will not advocate for your death. But neither will I stop anyone here who might desire it."

Saidhe had already turned her back on the drakes and was heading up the slope to be with Aurora. Brigit waited until the youngling was safely out of the Great One's range and then gave Tezcatlipoca a last, almost playful squeeze. "Behave yerself, laddy," she added, as she released him. "Next time, A might not be so charitable."

The Great One shifted onto his haunches with the dignity of an affronted cat, then looked from Brigit to Grishka and back again. "You will breed with him," he said, trading uncertainty for disbelief. When Brigit responded with an enthusiastic warble, he cocked his head and said, "Why him and not me? I was a god."

"Yer also an arsehole," Brigit said. "All ye had ta do to reconcile with tha drakena was apologize for pissing off tha Divine—"

"Apologize," Tezcatlipoca echoed, radiating incredulity.

"But no-o-o!" she went on. "You dragged the estrangement out fer three fecking ages and then thought ta kick off the fourth by turning younglings inta fecking incubators. That's why not you!" She turned to Grishka then and added, "A'm thinking tha maybe A might want ta kill him after all."

Grishka shrugged. "Your choice."

Tezcatlipoca chose to ignore that exchange. "So," he said to Grishka. "You apologized." Grishka nodded. "And now you are reconciled." Grishka nodded again. "Does that reconciliation apply to all? Or is it exclusive to you?"

"Only the Divine can say, Great One," Grishka replied. "Perhaps you should ask Her."

"Perhaps I will," Tezcatlipoca said. "Perhaps—" He lapsed into silence, pursuing that 'perhaps' perhaps. When he returned from his chase, he started as if surprised to see everyone still here.

"Go away now, Grishka," he said, "and take your circus with you. I have things to do."

EPILOGUE

The New Year's Eve party at Max and Mara's was a family affair. Appetizers studded every available flat surface; champagne and Scotch were the beverages of choice. Dick Clark mugged for the cameras on the big screen TV and counted down the minutes until 2012.

"Year of The Dragon," Roz noted, toasting with Max. "We made it. Thank you, Jesus." She speared a pot sticker with a thumbnail and then popped the dumpling in her mouth. As she mmmmphed-mmmmphed it down, Max made a face and said, "Very becoming. Did you learn that from Brigit?"

"I believe I was an accomplished slob before I met Brigit of The Sacred Flame and The Hearth," Roz said, deliberately talking with her mouth full. "So, no. She cannot claim credit for my table manners or lack thereof." She treated him to a devilish grin and added, "Would you like me to show you something she did teach me?"

He forestalled her with an upraised hand. "Thanks," he said, "but as you know, I have a delicate constitution." He took a sip of Scotch and then gave into his curiosity. "Is she going to join us tonight?"

Roz laughed as if she had never heard such a funny question. "Not a chance! She and Grishka dove into Lake Siskiyou the second after we got there and have yet to come up for air." In a less amused tone, she added, "As far as I'm concerned, she can stay down there until her once-an-age itch is satisfied. Because frankly, there are some things in this world that I don't want to experience."

Max waggled his eyebrows and said, "You say that now."

"Yes, I do," she replied, and then butted in on the conversation Mara and Aurora were having about the new house. "It's going to be palatial, Mar!" she said. "A wing for me, a wing for Mom, a wing for any dragons who happen to be in the neighborhood, and an Olympic-sized swimming pool!"

"Are you going to stock the pool?" Max quipped, only half in jest. Mara elbowed him in the ribs, a love-tap for being a smart-ass, and then carried on with the discussion as if they had not been interrupted. "It sounds divine," she said. "When do you think you'll be able to move in?"

"The contractor says mid- to late-July," Aurora said, helping herself to a shrimp canape. "If we're lucky, that is. As Roz said, it's a big place."

"In the meantime, I hope you'll change your mind and move into our spare room," Mara said. "I hate the thought of you living all alone in downtown San Jose. It's not safe!"

Aurora let out a one-note laugh that had little to do with merriment. "After the year I've had," she said, "downtown San Jose seems pretty darn tame. And to be honest, I need a little time alone to get my life in order and my head on straight so I can start writing again."

"Woo-hoo!' Max cheered. "Here's to the next adventure of Esmerelda and Francine!"

"Wouldn't that be nice?" Aurora said, in a distant, wistful tone.

"And what about you, Missy? Mara asked, as Roz reached past her for the bottle of single malt. "When are you going to move back to the Bay Area? Don't you find it incredibly hard to be living so far away from your best friends?"

Roz laughed. "I cry into my pillow every night," she said, as she poured herself and then Max another splash of Scotch. "But I'm not ready to put Shasta behind me just yet. That mountain has a really intriguing vibe."

Max mocked her with finger quotes that he then pinched into the universal sign for dope-smoking. "Oooh, a 'vibe'. Sounds like someone's been spending her free time in Weed!"

"Shut up, Max," Mara said, but Roz took no offense. "I can't explain it any other way," she said, giving the ice cubes in her glass a thoughtful rattle. "There's just something about that mountain that fascinates me."

"Sadie says there's magic there," Aurora remarked.

Before Max could make another marijuana joke, Mara pounced on the chance to change the subject. "I can't believe that little dickens didn't want to join us tonight. I thought we were friends."

"Don't feel bad," Aurora said. "She wasn't snubbing you. She was snubbing Naga."

Max made a rude noise. "Do you know how that drakena RSVPed to the invitation we sent her?" He paused for effect and a swig of whiskey, then said, "She sent Lee over to tell us never to contact them again. Hell! We were just trying to be friendly!"

Mara snatched the glass from his hand and wordlessly replaced it with a bottle of water. Then she returned her attention to Aurora. "What's Sadie's problem with Naga? I thought they got along OK."

"More than OK, apparently," Aurora replied. When Mara pressed her with an and-then look, she added, "Naga wants to take Sadie under her wing—so to speak. In fact, she's offered to teach her and all of her rescued clutch-mates the things that young dragons ought to know."

"Sounds like a pretty good deal," Mara said. "What's the catch?"

"The catch," Aurora said, "is that we probably wouldn't see too much of each other ever again." When Mara sucked in a breath, vicarious pre-separation anxiety, Aurora hastened to put the worst of her fears to bed. "Oh, we'll still share a bond, that's life-long. But she'd have to stay with Naga while she's training, and Lee says some of her lessons are fifty years long. That's not a lot of time for a dragon. But it is—"

"For you," Mara said, doing that math in her head. "So, you don't want her to go?"

Aurora took a sip of champagne and then said, "I want what's best for her. And what's best for her is her choice to make."

"So, Sadie doesn't want to go," Mara concluded.

"She's on the fence, actually. But she doesn't like to be rushed. When Naga pushes—and you know she does—Sadie instinctively pushes back. She needs the freedom to decide on her own."

"Wow," Max said, less obnoxious now that he had been warned and hydrated. "You're really going to stand back and let the chips fall where they may? I don't know if I could do that. I'm not sure I have the strength."

"I've had some practice at it," Aurora said, casting Roz a look that was both loving and pointed. "But as irksome as the process may be, I do have to say that the results are turning out beautifully." She raised her champagne glass, inviting the others to do likewise. "Here's to 2012, The Year of the Dragon. Here's to the start of a new age."

"Here, here!" they all said in unison. "Here, here!"